NOW AND FOREVER FREE

SEDUCTION IN RED, WHITE & BLUE

SUBIRA MILES

Hun Bun Luv
Publishing
SWEET TREATS FOR THE HEART

NOW AND FOREVER FREE: SEDUCTION IN RED, WHITE, AND BLUE
Copyright © 2024 HUN BUN LUV PUBLISHING

Cover Designed by Iesha Bree of IB Designz www.ibdesignz.com

Edited by V. Rena of Red Diamond Editing reddiamondediting5@yahoo.com

DEDICATION

For all the fan club girlies who used artist posters as décor, collected special edition magazines, watched music video premieres, and loved fan fiction.

SYNOPSIS

Graham Ward, known as 'G-Style,' is a teen pop star turned grown and sexy R&B singer whose lyrics glorifying skinny women have landed him in trouble with the popular blogger 'MsThickChickRevolutionary.' The new Spinner Records CEO demands that G-Style fix his PR problem by appearing with a full-figured woman. Graham disagrees until he runs into the elusive Jasmine Myers, at an industry awards show.

Actress Jasmine Myers is faithful to a fault, even when her professional basketball player fiancee is not. When his actions cause her career to crumble, Jasmine has finally had enough. She's learned her lesson: no more celebrity relationships... or maybe just one.

PROLOGUE

NOW - JULY 4TH FREEDOM AWARDS SHOW FOR BLACK EXCELLENCE

Jasmine

Classless. That's what my Aunt would say. She'd probably throw in *harlot* and *loose*, too. She could be right. Getting fucked on the wall of a bathroom probably qualified me for those titles, but I didn't care. For him, I'd be that. I'd take it wherever, however, from him, and it felt amazing.

The fourth of July, and this beautiful man was trying to find his freedom in the bottom of my pussy. I couldn't be mad at him because he was literally doing a stand-up job. With every thrust, he inserted more and more thoughts of a future with him and blurred remnants of my past.

We were supposed to be in our seats at the Twenty-Eighth Annual Freedom Awards, celebrating Black Excellence, but he was in *me*, giving me all of his excellence.

The Swarovski crystals on my soft, pink, rounded nails glinted against his brown shoulder as he pumped into me. Legs spread and feet locked at his back, he loaded into me with stroke after stroke.

"Stop holding back," I demanded in a sing-song voice, following the rhythm of his bouncing balls against the bottom of my ass. I didn't understand why he was trying to last and wouldn't let go.

Being a hoe for this man, who wanted to *be* my man, was glorious. Ten out of ten, he's recommended.

He responded with an extended backward move that caressed all sides of my insides before he dove back into my core.

"Give me my nut," I pleaded. I needed him to cum, to finish so that we could end this blissful torture.

"Say you're mine," he answered.

He lifted me, turned my face away from him, and then drove into me from the back.

I moaned but didn't answer as he picked up the pace and pressed my ass cheeks further apart before he drove in harder.

"Shit. Um…" I couldn't speak. The fact that my face was pressed tightly against the wall didn't help. It wasn't fair. He knew I loved the way that he plowed into me. He knew I loved it when he was *relentless*. I flexed my pelvic muscles, clamping my core around the base of his thick, veiny shaft—the *finish-him* move. The super play combo, widen, tighten, flex, and pull, usually rocketed us into pleasure explosions.

"J… Got damn. Quit playing," he growled but didn't stop his pursuit. No, he pistoned harder, making me mindless with bliss.

He was going to win. He was going to make me give in.

My nerve endings caught fire as he gripped my shoulder and clamped my waist, leaving no space inside of my canal. He took up all of it and all of me.

"Act like you fucking know," he punctuated each word with a rocket of hips into my center. "This my shit."

It was no lie. It was. That was more than I needed to explode into the highest splendor available on earth.

I shattered into rivulets of stars as he hooked his arms underneath mine to grab my breasts and grind harder.

His erratic breathing tickled my ear before he released a guttural growl that signaled the rise and fall of his climax.

"What if it doesn't work?" I asked between gulps of air against the wall. His legs held me up, but his torso held me down.

"We will always work if we both try," he said, disconnecting from me to reapply his clothing.

"What about the media? What about our careers?" I asked while searching for my dress, which I located on the counter.

I grabbed one of the cloth towels available, and I was thankful that this facility provided paper towels and washcloths in the private restroom.

I was finally free, and he was trying to change my status. He was trying to lock me down - again, tangle my life and career up with his. Can I choose me and have him, too? Can I have the job that I wanted and be his girl? Was it worth the scrutiny?

1

JASMINE

PAST - MONTHS BEFORE THE FREEDOM AWARDS SHOW FOR EXCELLENCE

www.celebritylifebuffet.net

Full-figured beauty and actress, Jasmine Myers, best known for her steamy love scene in the movie 'One Night Stand' and the 'boss bitch' attitude she brings to her roles, is the furthest thing from a boss when it comes to her relationship with basketball superstar, Dylan Simmons. Over the last two years, Dylan has had three paternity lawsuits filed against him and pictures of his privates posted by multiple alleged mistresses. All the while, Jasmine remains faithful, loyal, and extremely quiet concerning their relationship, often laughing off accusations of his unfaithfulness. She may be dense, but she is sure to be devoted.

-Staff Writer, Top Five Clueless Celebrities

The pressure in my chest expanded, constricting my throat. I gasped for air. It had happened. He had done it, and I felt it in the pit of my stomach, in the depths of my soul, and in the middle of my heart.

"No. Not again." I choked out.

I rechecked with a childish hope that maybe I had forgotten every skill I acquired in kindergarten and read the words searing through my phone completely wrong.

The words had to be wrong. Right?

"Dylan!" I belted out from the bottom of my gut as I hopped out of the bed and out of my bedroom in two leaps. "Dylan. Where are you?"

As usual, my new fiancé was missing in action. When had he left? Why had he gone?

It was probably guilt. Knowing Dylan, it was definitely out of guilt. He had messed up and slinked away before sunlight, realizing he'd be caught. Typical.

Barefoot and burning with anger, I stomped through my five-bedroom home, jerking open doors just to slam them shut, looking for the man I had agreed to marry. We were supposed to be happy. We were supposed to be in the best time of our relationship, and he was ruining it—our relationship, his image, and my acting career.

It had been this way between us for years now. Every time I took him back, I prayed it would be different. I hoped that he would leave the fragments of my healing heart intact. Not so.

"Dylan!" I yelled again, reaching the kitchen. I needed answers. His actions affected more than just him, and while he didn't suffer any consequences, I had.

"That's my ear." Peyton, my cousin and manager, winced. "If you were yelling at me like that, I wouldn't answer either."

In the kitchen, poised on a stool with a dainty cup of tea, she eyed my anxious pace across the tile floor.

"Peyton Lynn Prince, have you seen this?" She couldn't have. As part of my management team, Peyton couldn't have seen the damaging social media post about Dylan and me going viral.

I shoved my phone closer to Peyton's face as she placed her cup perfectly in the center of a saucer.

"Look…" I needed her to see it, confirm how bad it was, and devise a plan to fix it, doing what she did best.

"If you remove it from my eyeball, maybe I can examine it." Her voice remained smooth and steady as she gently glided my arm to the side and slid the phone from my hand.

My theatrics never fazed Peyton. No matter what I said or how I said it, she always seemed to be in a state of Zen.

Her eyes swept over the picture as I tapped the marble counter. Peyton didn't say anything, but I wanted to scream.

"Do you see it? Did you read it?" I step back into my pace pattern around her and the island. "Why the hell would he do that?"

I was literally going in circles around my kitchen and figuratively looping, a tailspin motion in my relationship.

Peyton pushed the glasses up on her nose and casually dropped the phone on the counter, unbothered.

"It's Dylan. Him sleeping in another woman's bed isn't new, Jasmine." She shrugged. "I'm surprised you still have the energy to get angry.

I bit my lip and tried not to shout. I tried to keep my emotions together, wrapped up tight like Peyton seemed to.

I looked at the post, a selfie of a woman dressed in a silk tank top beside a shirtless sleeping Dylan. The caption - *Not a punch was thrown, but he knocked the fuck out* - was annoying enough, but the fact that she tagged me before adding, - *Come get your man* - was the part that had me seeing red.

"Let me see her in the streets." I shook my head. "It's on sight, I swear."

Peyton stood up and took a few dainty steps to the kettle with her pink tea cup. "You haven't had a fistfight since second grade, Jas, and that was only three seconds long."

"Still. The disrespect." I reiterated.

"Disrespect from this random woman or the continued disrespect from the man you're supposed to marry?" Dipping a metal strainer of tea leaves into her cup, Peyton moved back to her seat without a glance in my direction.

I didn't have an answer for that. I never answered that question out loud. Peyton only paused before continuing.

"You should be concerned about the morals and adverse media clauses in the contract for Sacred Commitment." She sipped her tea.

"The studio was prepared for this possibility, even guarded themselves against it in your contract, but you seem surprised. There's a real chance that you may be let go from this role because you keep holding on to Dylan."

I didn't want to face her, but I heard her place the teacup down on the saucer—precisely in the center again, I'm sure. It would be too wrong for anything in her life to be unparalleled.

I needed more friends, new friends. The kind who agreed with you then hopped into a car to ride out at any moment. Peyton was more of a send-a-veiled-threat-in-an-email type of cousin, but she was right.

Peyton unceremoniously picked up the cup and sipped her tea without pressing for discussion.

I knew in my heart that when I signed the contract with the wholesome faith-based movie company, Dylan could mess it up for me. I didn't want to admit that to myself, but I knew. Conservative and wholesome Covenant Media & Movies needed to expand their diverse movies and wanted the award-winning Kema Bridges to direct a few exclusive streaming movies for them. Kema Bridges wanted me to be the lead. She believed in me that much. Covenant agreed to let me have a significant role, not the lead, with an addendum- no negative press surrounding infidelity. They were not taking any chances with image or profits because of me and my messy relationship history.

With a sigh, I collapsed onto the bar chair beside her, my head falling into my hands. I had been on an emotional rollercoaster with Dylan for so long that even the flat track seemed like a hill.

"I'm losing it." I only meant to think and feel those words, but I said them aloud.

The words never had to leave my lips for Peyton to know their truth. Dylan and his cheating had consumed my thoughts. It had consumed *me*. Every picture, every text, and every action he made, I was constantly trying to read between the lines and figure out the truth before the truth knocked on my door with a court order for a paternity test.

"It is what it is right now, but you don't have to keep going through this." Peyton's voice held more comfort than disappointment. "Kema or the studio will contact you if a decision is made about the role. Let's focus on your schedule for now." She gave a half smile and patted my shoulder.

"The Film Excellence Awards ceremony is tonight, and you know Tisa Sparks is running the show."

"How could I forget?" I winced. "That woman is scary."

"Yet very effective." Peyton's admiration beamed in her eyes as she spoke about the tall, no-nonsense executive producer. "But you know the rules: All four people at your table must be present to be seated, or you lose your 'in camera range' location."

"Right." I looked at my cell phone, my stomach anxiously twisting. Dylan still hadn't responded to my texts and calls from earlier. Him, his teammate, and his teammate's wife were supposed to dine with us at the table I scored.

I had messed up. I had involved Dylan in too much of my business life, which continuously backfired.

"There's a promo event for your role in *Brazen Renegade* with Bizzy Brian tomorrow."

"I thought you were trying to cheer me up." I groaned. "Anything to do with Brian is annoying."

"Being booked should make you happy."

It did. I enjoy what I do for a living, but I couldn't keep lying to myself about Dylan weighing down my progress to rise.

As if sensing my growing emotions, Peyton reached for both hands and squeezed my fingers.

"This is it, Jasmine." She spoke the words with certainty. "This is what we've worked so hard for."

I looked away from her, pushing down memories of us playing out lines all night and blitzing to auditions across state lines in the small car we shared. I pushed down the flashbacks of our panic to get back to campus for her college midterms after a long shoot. Peyton had been there with me, even when Dylan wasn't.

The lump in my throat held the word that my nod implied.

"You have to focus, Jas. We're at the start of the Olympics, and we've been running with the JV squad. We're in the big time." She explained. "Don't let Dylan get in the way of your victory, of what we have worked so hard for."

The soft thud of a forming headache reminded me how hard that might be.

2

GRAHAM

G-Style used to be my favorite R&B artist, but his new song "Right Girl" has the wrong message. The line, "She needs a one-digit figure if she wanna make me bigger," not only reinforces unrealistic beauty standards but also implies that a woman's value is tied to her size. It's damaging and exclusionary, sending the message that only skinny girls are worthy. Daily, women are shamed for their bodies, but music and media exacerbate stigmas of inadequacy. Beauty comes in all shapes and sizes, and no one should be made to feel lesser because of their body type. It's time for artists to embrace inclusivity and celebrate diversity in all its forms. Let's challenge these harmful stereotypes and demand music that uplifts and represents all women, regardless of their size. Do better, G-Style.

-Miss Thick Chick Revolutionary, Thick Thighs & Uncovering Lies

I hated meetings. I hated questions. I hated meetings that were full of questions even more. There hadn't been a meeting at Spinner Entertainment yet where solutions happened. Real ideas happened through open dialogue - on sofas or in cafes with friends. My most brilliant thoughts happened right before deep sleep when my mind was free. Where they didn't happen was staring in the face of bored businessmen who made decisions about music that they didn't understand. I had survived four new label executives, and if the current newbie was anything like the last, the meeting would end the same: them presenting exaggerated fears, me annoyed, while they were threatening to take away my livelihood if I didn't follow their vision. I made them a lot of money, troubled or not, and at this point, they needed me more than I needed them.

"Let's make this a good meeting," Kingston, my longtime manager, commented as we approached the conference room door.

After Miss Thick Chick Revolutionary, host spots, appearances, and brand promotions decided to part ways with me, people insinuated that I didn't like big girls, and sponsors started looking at me sideways. Suddenly, my image may not be the right fit for their venue.

The oval table boasted the record label's who's who. Everyone was there, including the crisis management team assembled when I had a scuffle with a reporter two years ago.

Was my comment situation that critical? No one had gotten injured—maybe a few feelings, but no bodily harm.

Someone always asked me questions about my behavior. The annoying part was that most of those passing judgment had done the same or worse.

"Social media says you, G-Style, have been canceled."

A collective of disapproving groans swelled as heads turned in my direction.

"So." I shrugged.

"Well," a smart-looking guy, who always had a number to report, spoke up. "Women ages 25 to 45, your target base, associate you with negative feelings after the release of your song *Perfect Girl*. The statement about preferring women who wore dress sizes that contained one digit was viewed as the most problematic, along with your unwillingness to clarify or apologize for the statement."

The table members rotated their heads back to Mr. Sean Walton, who was leading the discussion.

"Why is it that women can discuss what they want in a man and even give out a specific inch requirement, but men can't have a preference?" I asked.

A few throats cleared, and heads trended downward.

"We're not here to debate the merits of your statement. We're here again to discuss your statement's damage to your public image." He retorted.

"Miss Thick Chick Revolutionary has sparked a cancellation outcry. Streaming sales have plummeted, and your music has been pulled from an upcoming Rom-Com movie soundtrack since it doesn't - and I quote, *inspire all women to love their whole selves.*"

Nods and grunts of agreement took off through the room.

"We need to figure out how to make it disappear." Numbers explained. "We can bury it in a slew of positive press to make people forget. We can slide a full-figured woman into a music video."

They were excited now, throwing out descriptors as though what I preferred had no place, hoping to get a gold star from their boss.

"No. No. Videos are too costly, and no one watches them anymore," Sean added. "Who can we get as arm candy for appearances?"

"I'm right here." I reminded the eager people before I rose to my full height. "I've never been about fake shit, and I won't start today. I'm a man of my word; you should be straight about yours. We already agreed on a budget that included two music videos for this project."

Despite his calm demeanor, I knew Sean was heated. He didn't lift his voice or body when he precisely cut through my words. Sean Walton, the grey-eyed, light-skinned, self-appointed *sisters-serenader*, was a few years older than me and forever been a hater, even when we were younger. We often toured in the same circuits as teen heart-throbs, and he always found a way to try and upstage me. He even tried to get the same women that I had, and succeeded with a few. Not much had changed nearly twenty years later, except he had a CEO title to boost his ego.

"That's before we had to spend money on PR to clean up this

mess. If you want to continue with Spinner, you will listen and abide by what I say." His eyes narrowed. Walton never let his stare stray from mine, and if he thought I would flinch, he was misinformed. I wasn't some lost skinny teenager anymore competing for label attention and fan adoration. His title didn't mean shit to me.

A hush fell over the room as the excitement of new ideas dissipated into an eerie nervousness. "Is that an order?" I asked.

He didn't answer, which was what I thought would happen.

"Are you putting your foot down?" I inquired.

Crickets. The man said nothing, but I could tell by his tense jaw muscles that he was most likely grinding his teeth.

"Don't cross me, Graham." He ground out the words as if he had to restrain himself, but I wanted him to leapfrog his weak ass my way and give me a reason to lay him out.

"Oh, well, excuse me as I step around you then," I responded before moving toward the door.

I left the meeting without glancing back at Kingston or anyone who felt they had any control over what I did with my life.

Before I made it out of the building, my cell phone rang.

"Fuck their contract," were the first words out of my mouth. It was Kingston. Even though he was the manager, we treated each other like family, so there was no need to bother with a greeting.

"That's part of why you and the Young Guyz still owe Spinner an album." Kingston hadn't been my manager then.

The boy band my uncle and I put together, started and ended when I was an adolescent, still owed Spinner an album—one that I never planned to complete. I still had one project on the outrageous twelve-album deal I signed as a very young solo artist too many years ago. The last album, *Finally Free*, was scheduled to drop during the Freedom Awards for Black Excellence during the Fourth of July holiday, where I'd receive a spotlight award.

I was tired of the label, but Kingston was the only man I respected enough to talk to me like that. He always kept it honest.

Ten years older than me, he often felt like a big brother, a father, or a friend, depending on the situation.

"You've got bigger things to deal with than a blogger." He added.

I half muttered, "I know," as I thought about my responsibilities.

The weight of knowing all the things that sat on my shoulders pushed my temper down a little. I would have to suck it up. People depended on me. My parents, Kingston, barber, chef, charities, the list was endless, much longer than my energy and patience.

Kingston could smell a win on the horizon and quickly said, "I'll meet up with the execs and nail down a plan that works for everyone."

"If they want me to do this, talk to them about a budget for a video shoot," I added before reminding him of my non-negotiables and ending the call.

3

JASMINE

Dear valued audience,

We understand that recent developments regarding one of our cast members, Jasmine Myers, have caused concern and speculation. We hold our artists to high standards of conduct and integrity on and off the screen. We are carefully evaluating the situation surrounding her involvement in our upcoming film. We recognize the importance of maintaining our company's values. Our priority remains delivering quality entertainment that aligns with our audience's expectations. We appreciate your patience as we navigate this matter with diligence.

-Covenant Movie & Media Company, Press Announcement

Walking the red carpet at The Film Excellence Awards should have been a breeze. I had a new movie ready to debut on screen in a few weeks. I had appeared in several films the previous year, and people still tagged me in commentary about my role in the sexy thriller, *One Night Stand*. There were things to talk about. There were topics to discuss relating to my career, but of course, that woman chose the devil's work instead. I was minding my own pretty-girl business when daytime show host, Madison Humphries, slithered her old ass over to me on the red carpet for a quick interview. Intuition told me to keep it moving. Madison meant no good to anyone, but it was a beautiful day with beautiful people, so maybe she could take a day off from being miserable. No, today, misery had company, and she was working overtime.

I was convinced that hateful hack had no friends in real life, and that's why she constantly sought to destroy mine. If any celebrity looked happy, that woman would find some dirt to kick up about them. Trouble in life or a relationship? She would exploit and stretch the heartache as an opportunity for her to be seen with her loud-ass opinion.

I swallowed down about six curse words. The Film Excellence Awards was a classy event in a ballroom connected to an expensive, overpriced, high-rise hotel. I couldn't go off on her like I wanted, so I gathered a plastic smile and answered her rude question.

"My character Trixie in the movie *Brazen Renegade* is all about getting things done, even if it means doing it alone. I'm a woman who knows how to make things happen and look good while doing it." That was my response to reporter Madison Humphries and her shady question about why I was walking the red carpet alone.

"Uh-huh." She nodded and motioned for the assistant to come near with her phone. "I see you arrived dressed appropriately for the Golden Age of Hollywood theme. You're wearing a black chiffon and lace Diaisha Blayse gown, right?"

"I am," I proudly stated while wondering what the woman was looking up on her phone. "I love supporting black women designers, who tailor garments to fit women with a lot of body and confidence."

"That makes sense. No one could deny that you have a whole lot of body." Madison added a slight lilt to her voice that made her words sound sweet or happy when they were not. "The dress was just as stunning on the model Jubilee when she wore it to a gala last year."

Madison lifted her phone to the camera and showed it to me with an expectant smirk.

Before I could tear that muppet-looking, fish-eyed donkey down with a few choice words, the director, Kema Bridges, moved me to the side.

"They wear it well." Kema stated before adding, "And all of the juicy girls with curves are thankful for models like Jubilee and actresses like Jasmine who show up on walkways and in movies, representing when media wants us to throw on a bedsheet for clothing, sell household goods in commercials, or be the lonely best friend in movies. Shoutout to Jasmine for keeping it sexy and amazing in all her roles."

With that, Kema ushered me down the rest of the walkway, avoiding any more conversations with reporters as we waved them off with smiles and a hurried walk.

Brutal. The day had been absolutely terrible, and it wasn't improving.

"Where's Peyton? Are you alright?" Kema asked when we made it into the event center. The hallway was abuzz with people, cameras, and decorations. Wall to wall, well-to-do groups were chatting, so no one noticed the corner where Kema and I took up residence.

"No," I took a deep breath, held my back, and fanned my face as I fought to keep tears from falling. The last thing I needed to do was mess up my makeup and be caught looking a mess for public embarrassment. "Peyton stayed behind so Dylan could come with me, but him all over the internet, the movie role in jeopardy, and Madison talking shit, I'm on edge."

Saying the words out loud made them all the more real and sharpened the pain pinging in my chest.

"Don't freak out," Kema soothed. "The executives are meeting as we speak, and they'll let me know soon."

That made me want to cry even more. Kema Bridges, the director of the movie I may not get to participate in, had convinced the company to take a chance on me, and Dylan was messing up her project.

"Did you read their press announcement?" I whined. "It sounded like they've already made a decision."

Kema looked concerned. We had worked together when she was an assistant on a show where I played a crazy ex-girlfriend who stalked one of the main characters. We have been amenable since.

A beep rang out over the loudspeaker before an announcer spoke, "Everyone, please take your seats. The show will begin shortly."

"I'll let you know as soon as I know." Kema hugged me. "My group is going in, and the production around here plays no games about seats."

We air-kissed, and she skittered along to catch up with her group.

I turned to the entrance, hoping against all hope that this man would show his ass in the building rather than all across social media. It was embarrassing enough to walk the red carpet alone, but I would get bumped from the front of the room table if I didn't have my entire party ready to be seated.

I searched the hallway, noticing how the room had thinned out quickly. Everyone joined up to enter the ballroom. I was alone again, waiting, wondering why I kept Dylan around.

After a few minutes, another announcement and less than five people standing in the hallway, Tisa Sparks, the no-nonsense producer, headed my way.

I shivered. That woman was scary. She had to be over six feet tall without heels. She was solidly built with straight hips, a thin waist, full breasts, and a surprise backside that looked like the basketballs she should be dribbling.

Tisa's voice was as big as her butt, so when she stepped over to me, clipboard in hand, and asked, "Do you have an ETA on Dylan Simmons so that we can get you seated?" I jumped a little.

"Uh," I stalled, darting my eyes toward each entrance, hoping he would walk in. "No."

She didn't seem sympathetic when she said, "We won't be able to hold your front-row table, so we'll fill those seats at table eight and place you at table sixty-seven."

My hope drowned, so I barely paid attention to Tisa as she spoke into the headset microphone and moved away. I wanted to be mad at her, but a tiny bit of admiration built in the back of my mind. Tisa was so focused, decisive, and not for the bull shit - the opposite of me. How much further along would I be in my career if I wasn't constantly being pulled in different directions by Dylan's never-ending stream of distractions?

I was hoping that something would go right, that I could catch one break. Dylan knew how much the positive press from this event meant to me. And yet, once again, he managed to let me down.

The slight sound of the automatic doors swooshing open caught my attention. When I saw *him*, my heart leaped, wanting to break free of my body.

It was Graham "G-Style" Ward, the finest man on this side of the universe. He looked like the kind of trouble that would fuck out a girl's insides but leave her filled with pleasure.

Only holy intervention could have granted me the privilege of his eyes drifting over me and perusing my body. The way he looked me up and down with intrigue blazing in his gaze almost made me believe he liked thick girls.

He winked in my direction, and I almost fainted.

My breath caught in my throat, and my pulse quickened. Graham may never like me, but G-Style would forever be my schoolgirl crush. I couldn't tear my eyes away from him, and my mind must have believed that he didn't want to let go of my sight either.

Tisa Sparks broke up the moment, grabbing G-Style's attention.

"Let's get your party seated, Mr. Ward," she told him before I was there, alone, again.

4

GRAHAM

Tiddies. That's all I saw at first; they were great, big, round ones that looked like they could nourish a whole neighborhood. Her tapered waist fed into full curvy hips that could handle all of my 6'3 solid frame. I stared at Jasmine like a teen left overnight with all the cable channels staring at the television. Unblinking because, dammit, she deserved all the admiration.

She was fucking gorgeous, and I couldn't keep my eyes off her. She still looked like the same girl I was mesmerized by in the music videos, but she was all grown up and, exponentially, a woman. Short, loose curls bracketed her oval face, brushing her dimpled chin. Thick, bubble-licious lips, almond-shaped expressive eyes and nicely angled cheekbones had me wondering how I could get closer to her.

Like on the big screen, she stood out, and I needed to sit near her.

"Get me at Jasmine's table," I said.

Kingston shook his head before frowning.

"I'm not a genie," he retorted. "There's assigned seating, and the table where Jasmine sits is way back there. That's the non-compliance table."

"The what?" I was baffled. I'd never heard of a non-compliance table and didn't care about the seating arrangements. "What's a non-compliance table?"

"If they didn't have their entire group together by production set up, they get moved," Kingston explained. "Looks like her man didn't show up."

Sounds typical of the ignorant motherfucker. If Jasmine was my girl, there's no way I'd leave her open to be swooped up by another man. I'm showing up every time.

"Switch with her then," I stated. "Tell her to come up here, and you sit back at the non-compliance table."

"Man, hell no. This production team is serious. I can't go switching plans." He looked around before whispering the rest. "Tisa Sparks would take me out."

I already didn't want to be there. I only attended because Kingston begged me to, and the coordinator of music for visual productions and his wife would be at the table, not Sean Walton, the terrible CEO.

"Make it happen or I'm out." I meant it, too.

"This is what we're doing now? You're throwing tantrums?"

I looked at Jasmine chewing on that nice plump lip, then back to Kingston.

"For her, hell yeah."

Kingston eyed me briefly before huffing, sliding back, and walking off.

"Will everyone please remain seated? Five minutes until the show starts."

Shit. What if she said no? What if production escorted our asses out for not following directions? I can't have any more bad press.

Doesn't matter. I was willing to risk it for Jasmine. She's finally not attached to that bum, and I needed to take my chance.

My phone chimed, reminding me that I needed to put it on silent before they confiscated it.

Kingston- *This is messed up. You're kicking me to the curb for a girl.*

Me- *Nah, for a real ass woman.*

If she wanted me, I'd make her mine without a second thought. Jasmine had been that girl since she was sixteen and landed a gig on a popular soap opera. I had followed her career and how she moved for a long time—from afar. If she hadn't connected with college basketball phenom Dylan Simmons early in her career, I'd bet money that our status would be different now. His absence gave me hope that their status had changed.

I was so caught up in my response and thoughts that I hadn't noticed that the chair wasn't empty anymore.

I smelled her perfume first. Happy. If happy was a scent, it now belonged to her. I'm not sure how someone can smell like a feeling, but her scent was floral and light and lifting. She smelled like *joy.*

"Jasmine," I whispered. Her name was almost reverent in the way it left my lips.

There she sat, and I was tongue-tied. Speechless. I never understood how tight people got when meeting me, but it all made sense at that moment. She was everything I had imagined, and so many things I couldn't fathom, breathing the same air in the chair next to me.

Her smile widened.

"Are you alright?" She chuckled a little, and it was the best sound I'd ever heard.

I wanted to record her laugh and mix it with a jazzy saxophone over a thumping bass line to repeat. She had me thumping, low and deep.

I was falling fast, and she'd only said three words.

"Graham, right?" she asked, placing a hand on my shoulder.

I looked at her slim fingers and long nail beds with metallic gold paint and then gave her a grin that I knew was goofier than the cartoon character. Most people knew who I was but hearing her say my name warmed me.

"Would you mind sitting with me?" I asked cautiously, but the slight crack in my voice during the last words was new. I was nervous. I didn't want to look stupid in front of the girl I never stopped fantasizing about, who always seemed out of reach, and was finally closer than ever.

"Countdown to live," the announcer said through the speaker system.

"I'm not sure if I have a choice at this point," she teased me, and I smiled.

The music swelled slowly as the announcer called out each number from ten to three. Cameramen flooded the floor and stage, and two men seated on devices hovered above us with more cameras.

The lights dimmed, and famous people took the stage for everyone to see, but I wanted to watch her.

5

JASMINE

Chrysanthemums. That's all it took. Graham said the word chrysanthemums, and my body was ready to water a garden full of them. I almost moaned out loud in front of a table full of strangers. We had only been sitting there a few minutes when I noticed him eying the flower centerpiece. I watched him reach out and graze the tips of a petal. I'd never wanted to be a flower in my entire life, but in that moment, I wished that my legs were stems and my pussy was a petal.

"Beautiful," he murmured so low that I doubt the oblivious couple across from us even noticed.

"You like flowers?" I asked, catching his gaze when he turned to acknowledge me.

He pulled that bottom lip between his teeth for a second, making it look like he wanted to nibble on me. Then he tore his attention away, giving that amazing grin to the plants. He almost looked embarrassed, like he hadn't expected me to notice.

"I love flowers, especially chrysanthemums," he answered. "Did you know there are thirteen common types of chrysanthemums?"

I was amazed by G-Style. I had seen him on stage dancing like he needed a roof over his head, singing like he needed food in his belly, and grinding on women like he wanted to make a baby, but I would have never guessed that he loved flowers.

"How do you know so much about flowers?" I asked him when a crew dressed in black hurriedly moved across the stage. "That's an interesting talent."

His eyes fell against mine like I was his flower, a centerpiece decorating his vision. I think that I made the man blush.

"It's not a talent for real," he smirked. "My mom was heavy into interior design and kept fresh flowers around the house. I used to help her with arrangements."

I was amazed at the way his mouth moved. The sounds that came from between his lips made the show even better. Graham could say just about anything, and it would make me melt. I was trying to get my brain together and wrap my mind around my teenage dream of being less than a foot away from him, looking better than any vision I had made up.

After speaking to Graham, I realized that the awards show held no value. I barely knew who was on stage and couldn't repeat more than two words a presenter said. I waited for the stage breaks—the times set aside for set changes and commercials. With each stage break, Graham turned his attention to me.

As the lights dimmed to black after another award was given, a swarm of people in all black flooded the stage, and an army of white-shirt-black-vested servers covered the banquet room floor with silver trays.

Graham leaned over so close to me that his curly hair brushed my cheek, cool and soft.

"Time for the food," he whispered near my neck. Maybe he wanted to be heard over the clang of trays or set compiling; the reason would never matter. Him in my space had become my new favorite memory, and him pulling away as the server placed the menu card and plate down was now the saddest. "I can't wait to see what they're serving this year."

"Silken strands of artisanal pasta entwined with vibrant tomato essence, crowned with freshly grated Parmigiano-Reggiano," I read aloud. "Served with a butter-kissed baguette infused with garlic essence, whispering promises of indulgence."

Frowning, I looked at my plate, re-read the description in my mind, and then met Graham's waiting gaze.

"Spaghetti," we said at the same time. Our simultaneous laugh could compete with my joy when drinking a milkshake.

"I can't believe their definition of an elevated gastronomical experience is the after-church special," I commented.

"All that's missing is the extra crispy catfish fillet," he chuckled.

"You went to Hilltop Community Baptist, too?" I knew he didn't, but for a long time, I thought catfish and spaghetti were something my aunt made up since no one who wasn't associated with her cooked them that way.

"Nope, but I swear my grandmother's church stayed serving catfish and spaghetti plates for five dollars every week."

"I just hope I don't get any on me or my clothes," I added before eyeing the plate of food. "My clothes haven't survived a battle with spaghetti yet."

"I'm trying to see you win," he laughed. "What do you need from me? An extra napkin? Do you want me to feed you?"

The way his voice lowered and his eyes darkened when he asked the last question had my mouth dry because my pussy stole all the water my body had to offer. I wondered if he wanted to feed me the spaghetti or something else. I was willing to choke on anything he wanted to put in my mouth.

"I can handle it," I responded before adding, "I hope."

My water levels, nervous system, and dress all survived G-Style during the following awards presentations and performances. During the stage break, I returned to the somewhat neutral topic of flowers.

"This is such a beautiful flower setting," I stumbled over my words when he gave me his attention and winked. "I- I love flowers.

I buy fresh bouquets at home and have twelve succulent terrariums in my house."

"Succulents," he repeated the word before licking his lips. "I can see that."

To recap, the sexy words of the day, chrysanthemums and succulents, were brought to my attention by the letter F and the super word *me*. All I could think about was him fucking and sucking on me while I was splayed out across a bed of flowers. Could I be his succulent? Would he let me succulent him? The word had nothing to do with where my mind went but was on track for how giddy he made me feel.

"You'll have to show me yours one day, and I'll show you mine." He whispered, and I completely forgot what the fuck we were talking about.

I spun some spaghetti onto my fork, using a spoon to heap on some extra sauce because I needed something to do with my hands. Visions of Graham showing me precisely what he could do to mine pumped across my brain screen as I lifted the full fork.

At the same time, Graham leaned forward, close enough that the inhalation of his cologne could make me high enough to float away with him in my arms. That's when the inevitable happened - round twelve of me versus the spaghetti. I lost control of the fork. In slow motion, I watched as the utensil bounced on the table, and a glop of saucy noodles flew and landed on Graham's lap. It would have been the perfect paper towel commercial. I was sorely in need of a quicker picker-upper.

I beat the tomato-based meal for the first time, but it took out Graham's pants instead, leaving a red saucy trail down the front of the pants.

"Oh, no," I uttered too loud before I dabbed some water on my dinner napkin and went straight for Graham's crotch.

In the middle of my second swipe across his black pants and my third, "I'm so sorry," when the python he must have been carrying in his pocket woke up and wiggled for me.

"Jasmine," his voice was strained as he took my wrist to stop my cleaning efforts. "I got it."

"I'm so sorry," I pleaded, sitting up and preparing my body for the berating. How could I be so clumsy? I didn't take the time to think. That was so stupid of me. I should have known better. "I didn't mean for that to happen."

I couldn't even look at Graham. Dylan would have lit into me about paying attention. My aunt was relentless about cleanliness. She hated how clumsy I was and reminded me every chance she got.

"It's all good," Graham stated as he plopped the noodles from his lap onto the table. "No worries, they're only clothes."

The familiar tightening in my chest came first. I tried to take deep breaths, but they were all shallow.

Trapped. Graham was still rubbing at his pants when a whirlwind of fear slammed into me. I couldn't face him.

"Sorry," I murmured, grabbed my purse, whispered one more apology, and fled the table. I needed to get away before Graham was a casualty of me.

The announcer came back then. "We're live in 5,4,3 -" the music and lights changed.

I escaped through the door before security could lock the room again for taping. I had at least 15 minutes before Graham could exit. There was no movement during filming. Would he come after me, though? We didn't know each other. Would he send a cleaning bill or a lawsuit? I ruined his tuxedo and touched him.

Standing in a remote corner, as far away from the ballroom and stragglers as I could, I worked on slowing my breathing and soothing the panic. At least he had been gracious about it. Dylan would have made an enormous deal and had an attitude the entire night. It helped to soothe my nerves that he didn't seem fazed by it, but I was still embarrassed.

"Jasmine?" the voice startled me. I almost thought he escaped but turned to see Kema Bridges looking at me.

"Hey, Kema." I winced but tried to put on a fake smile.

"Are you alright?" she checked.

I nodded because I couldn't even force out a lie. Kema and I were at the workplace and on-set associates. We were grab-a-bite or a see-you-at-happy-hour cool, not telling you all my problems, besties.

"I hate to tell you this here," she began, and I read the disappointment in her eyes. "The studio has decided to remove you from the project."

It's one thing to believe something and assume the worst but to hear the air whooshing out of my lead-role-in-mainstream-movie aspirations in real time on top of all the other stuff was too much.

Kema went on, and I heard words but couldn't listen.

"I'm shopping around a great script for funding. I'm looking for investors, so I don't have to play their politics when hiring who I want."

I nodded absently. Kema was being nice. Who knew if she would ever get funded? I knew that Kema was sympathetic, but that didn't matter. I had lost the role.

She said something about keeping in contact and ended the conversation. My legs worked long enough to reach the empty employee restroom I had spotted in the back. It was large enough for me to fall apart in, and even though it was probably not the best place in the building, it still had marble floors, gold fixtures, a privacy stall around the toilet, and was extremely clean.

I locked the door behind me, and the weight of a tree trunk pressed against my chest.

They don't want me. No one wants me. The words echoed in my mind, each syllable carving more profoundly into the hurt.

Nobody wants me. The studio, the fans, my aunt, my parents—none of them thought I was worth holding onto. But Dylan did. He always came back to me. He always tried to love me even when he messed up. How sad was it that the only person in the world who wanted to keep me was a horrible human being?

Tears stung my eyes as I sank onto the floor, my heart heavy with disappointment and frustration.

Everything blurred together—my sad chant, the muffled sounds of people in the hallway, and the broken sobs that escaped my lips. I had anticipated the possibility of losing the role, but the reality of being fired because of Dylan's actions was a bitter pill to swallow. It wasn't fair.

It was hard to choose an emotion because I felt so many. Anger simmered as I replayed the events in my mind. Dylan, with his reckless behavior and selfish choices, had cost me more than just a job; he had sabotaged my career. And yet, I couldn't shake the nagging guilt twisting my gut. I had given him so much. How had I allowed him to hold such power over my life? How many times had I looked over his behavior while he walked over me and trampled over my heart?

All the tears I held prisoner for far too long flowed freely. They were a cascade of frustration and despair without caring about my location, dress, or professional makeup. Each sob was a painful reminder of the boundaries shattered, the pieces of me I let slip away. I was drowning, unable to pull myself over the tidal wave of disappointment. The regret of being lost in the idea of love and that I didn't ground my decisions on Dylan's actions all ate my confidence while adding weight to my despair.

6

GRAHAM

E ven if I had seen it in a crystal ball myself, I wouldn't have believed that Jasmine Myers would rub my dick and fall into my arms. Sure, spilled spaghetti and an emotional breakdown were the driving factors, but what relationship was perfect?

After I nearly burst through my pants when Jasmine lowered her body to slide a napkin over and around my lap, I knew for sure that there was something special brewing between us. A few touches from Jasmine had me ready to put her knees on my shoulders.

When she ran off, I got caught by the show starting and threatening glare of security.

As soon as I could, I entered the hallway, searching for any sign of Jasmine. She had disappeared without a trace, and despite my best efforts, the uneasy feeling stuck with me.

As I scanned the crowd, my gaze landed on Tisa, the formidable executive producer of the show, looking like someone's mama ready to snatch up a kid on punishment from a party. It was desperation that moved me to even approach her.

"Tisa," I greeted her, trying to add a layer of charm. "Have you seen Jasmine?"

Tisa's lips curved into a tight smile, her eyes gleaming with a hint of mischief. "Oh, I know exactly where she is," she replied cryptically. "But I'm afraid I can't divulge that information."

I'd heard that Tisa could be stubborn, but her refusal didn't deter me.

"This is an emergency. I need to make sure Jasmine is okay. She seemed upset earlier."

Tisa's expression softened slightly, and she tilted her head in contemplation. "Well, I suppose I could make an exception," she mused, her gaze narrowing. "But first, I need a favor from you."

"Name it," I replied.

Tisa's smile widened, and she gestured toward the tablet device that she cradled in her arm. After waking it up, she slid her hand across the screen. Images filled the page. She clicked on one of Jasmine and me looking like a couple. Then, she flipped through more before explaining the cost of her knowledge.

"I want permission to release stills of you and Jasmine at the dinner table, laughing and smiling together," she explained, her eyes glittering with anticipation.

I hesitated momentarily, weighing the consequences of agreeing to Tisa's request. The press had hounded Jasmine because of her sorry-ass man. I didn't want to add to that. I also didn't want to piss her off by agreeing to this. Tisa didn't necessarily need my permission to post the pictures somewhere, but I appreciated her being honorable in explaining how she planned to spin our seating arrangement. The image of Jasmine's radiant smile flashed before me, and I knew.

"Deal," I said firmly, meeting Tisa's gaze head-on. "Now, where is she?"

"Dang, I should have asked for exclusive film rights to the wedding," Tisa chuckled softly, her demeanor shifting as she relented. "She's in the small employee restroom to the left," she revealed, her tone gentler now. "She looked like she could use a friend."

With a sense of urgency propelling me forward, I hurried toward the restroom, my mind racing with a million different thoughts. But above all, I couldn't shake the hope that Jasmine hadn't felt embarrassed or offended by my actions.

My gut tightened, and I hesitated, pressing my ear to the door. A soft, heartbreaking sob met my ears, and without a second thought, I used the key that I bribed from a custodian, unlocked the door, and stepped inside.

There, Jasmine sat on the cold marble floor, her knees pulled up to her chest, her body was shaking with silent sobs.

She didn't look up as I entered or acknowledge my presence, lost in whatever storm had overtaken her. My heart ached to see her so vulnerable and alone. I wanted to ask her what was wrong, to fix whatever had broken her spirit. It wasn't about me. An accidental swipe wouldn't have someone tucked into themselves like a turtle. She was in pain, and the evidence of her hurt flowed from her eyes.

Instead, I quietly lowered myself to the floor beside her. The restroom was spacious and clean, with an enclosed toilet and gilded mirrors. It smelled nice and was highly upscale. The cold marble sent a shiver up my spine, but I ignored it, shifting until I sat beside her. I didn't say a word; I just scooted closer, our sides touching, offering my presence as a silent support.

Jasmine turned her head slightly, her tear-streaked face barely visible through the curtain of her hair. She didn't say anything; she just looked at me with eyes that seemed to hold the world's weight. I opened my arms, a silent invitation, and after a moment's hesitation, she leaned into me, her body collapsing against my chest.

I wrapped my arms around her, holding her close, feeling her sobs reverberate through both of us. Her tears soaked into my shirt, but I didn't care. I rested my chin on the top of her head, inhaling the faint scent of her shampoo, a mix of vanilla, fruit, and something uniquely Jasmine.

We just sat there for a while, the world outside the bathroom slipping away, leaving only the two of us in our bubble. I would wait as long as Jasmine wanted and hold her as long as she needed. I could feel the tension slowly draining from her body, replaced by a heavy exhaustion. I tightened my hold on her, hoping to show her that I wouldn't let go and that whatever was weighing her down, I could help lift her.

The sound of her breathing began to even out, her sobs turning into soft, shaky breaths. She didn't explain what had brought her to this point or offer clarification words, and I didn't push her. Sometimes, emotions couldn't be capsuled with words.

As the minutes ticked by, I felt her shift slightly, lifting her head to look up at me. Her eyes were red and puffy, but there was something there—a fragile, tentative hope, maybe even a flicker of gratitude.

I brushed a stray tear from her cheek, reassuringly smiling. She didn't return it, but the tightness in her expression eased a little, and that was enough for me.

We stayed there longer, the marble floor's cold seeping into our bones, but it didn't matter. All that mattered was that Jasmine wasn't alone and had someone to lean on, even for a little while.

The first time I saw her, she was auditioning for 'cute girl number two' in the Young Guyz video. She strolled in with her photos, attitude, and dance moves and strutted out with my attention and a vote for her in the role. The team didn't think she fit the profile of a video girl and chose someone else. I'd wanted to know her since. I finally got the opportunity.

"Thank you." Her voice was small.

"I needed to make sure you were alright," I said honestly. "I told you, I want to see you win."

Her lips trembled, and she looked up at me, her eyes glistening with unshed tears. "Win?" her voice cracked with emotion. "I've been losing so much lately that I'm not even sure what winning looks like."

I felt a lump in my throat. Tenderness was a side of Jasmine I'd never seen before. Jasmine was always the wise-cracking, sassy badass in her roles, and I didn't know if she shared this part of herself with many people. I was honored that she chose me.

"What do you need?" I asked.

Jasmine sat up, her hair matted, makeup smeared, and dress twisted, but she was everything I dreamed she would be and more.

"A strip tease, maybe?" She gave a weary half-smile, her eyes watering. "I would say I'm good, but I'm not." Her voice was filled with a vulnerability that tightened my chest. "I should be asking you what I can do for you."

I hated the pleading in her voice, the uncertainty that being cared for was attainable—something she had no right to. I wanted to change that.

I stood up and moved to the center of the small room. I toed out of my shoes, untucked my shirt, and unbuttoned my collar.

"I did hear that a strip show is also good for the spirit."

"I was playing." She choked out the words. I couldn't tell if it was a look of horror or surprise as she gave a watery laugh.

"Anything to bring back that smile -" I made a syncopated beat with my throat, pumped my hips, and opened up a few more buttons.

"Wait, no. I wasn't serious." She covered her eyes, but her smile spread.

"Nope. No request go unanswered." I continued bouncing and thrusting my hips toward her. "You've unleashed Mr. Beast, and he won't be tamed."

The belly laugh that rolled out of her made me chuckle, too. The curves of her cheeks almost covered her eyes when she let out a giggle and snort combination that I wouldn't have thought possible.

"What was that?" I marveled.

She snorted a laugh again before saying, "I can't help it, that's the corniest shit I've ever heard. Mr. Beast?"

I gave a playful pout before shrugging and saying, "Ah well, cuddles it is then."

"Yes, please." She laughed. "Being in your arms is everything right now."

She was serious when I looked at her. Her words massaged tender spots of emotions beneath my surface. Sex. That's all anyone ever wanted from me - to fulfill their fantasy of the hot guy with super sex. I made money from selling that fantasy, but I was glad Jasmine seemed to see beyond it.

It was like a ginger ale to an upset stomach, the brand name kind, when she invited me to her.

"Come talk to me," she paused. "Or don't, but I could use some comfort right now if you're willing to share."

"In here, still?" I asked, looking around the room again.

Jasmine looked wearily at the door as tears made free fall leaps from her face.

"Just a little longer," she swallowed hard as she sniffled again. "I'm not ready to face the world right now."

I wrapped my arms around her and pulled her in close to me. She fit against me perfectly.

Her soft, "Why?" caught my attention.

She pushed her gaze up to search mine. I could make out the confusion and maybe a piece of longing blink in her eyes.

"Why what?" I needed clarification.

"Why do you care?" She almost sounded like she would cry again. "Why bother checking on me when the one who caused all this chaos couldn't be bothered?"

I didn't know what to say for a moment. I hadn't anticipated this question. Finding the right words to convey the depth of my feelings was difficult.

"I've heard the stories about Dylan and read what they wrote about him and you." I caressed her shoulder as I spoke. "You deserve more than that bullshit. Something about you called out to me."

Her sadness was thick in the air between us. I searched my mind for something that might bring the smile back to her face. I hated the way that she wore sadness. It didn't fit her bright eyes or dimpled face.

"Hey," I began tentatively, "let me tell you a story."

Slowly, Jasmine nodded as she folded her arms around me and snuggled closer, her ear landing directly against my chest.

"As long as I can listen like this," she agreed.

I took a deep breath, gathering my thoughts before launching into the tale. "My mom is the real calm type. Not much rattles her. She's the picture of stoic, non-emotion, but this time, I saw her yell at the screen like she knew the characters personally."

I broke down the memory of my mom asking me to watch a movie with her one rainy afternoon.

"In the movie, Danny, I think was his name, had stolen your character's money, disappeared, and left your character to clean up the mess. Of course, he was mean and terrible before he left, and I think my mom could relate to that somewhat," I shook my head. It was a terrible moment for men everywhere. "I watched her face light up at that man's pain when he became ill, and you were the only person in the world that the hospital could find to take care of him. She cheered when you showed that man no mercy whatsoever. You would have thought she was in church the way she shouted for you."

I could feel Jasmine's laugh through her body.

"You gave his ass hell for a good third of the movie," I recalled, a smile tugging at the corners of my lips. "She loved your character and laughs every time she sees a spatula because you beat that man in the face with one after he spit out your food. It was like she found a piece of herself in that character, a spark of hope that anything was possible."

I glanced down at Jasmine, wanting to see hope reflected in her eyes. "My mom still watches that movie whenever she's pissed at my dad," I continued. "I asked her why it was her favorite movie. She told me it's a reminder that no matter how tough things get, she can stand up for herself - take control of her destiny."

I gently squeezed Jasmine's hand, my voice softening with sincerity. "I see that same strength in *you*, Jasmine—that same fire and determination. And I don't want you to lose that hope, that belief in yourself. Because you deserve to feel like you can conquer anything - to know that you can overcome all this bullshit."

My words didn't feel strong enough. I wanted to give a *Remember the Titans*, we're-a-team-and-we're-going-to-win kind of speech. An all-hope-is-lost, half-time talk that encouraged her to go out and win it all. I wanted to see her victory over whatever had taken her down.

"Why?" she repeated, her voice trembling with emotion. "I don't understand why you're being so kind to me."

"Because you're worth it. A gem that, under pressure, only got more amazing," I whispered, brushing a stray tear from her cheek. It bothered me that genuine kindness seemed foreign to her. "Because you're stronger than you know and deserve to be treated with kindness and respect, no matter what."

I saw a hint of fight in Jasmine's eyes, a flicker of belief that things could get better. And in that moment, I knew that I would do whatever it took to help her find her way back to happiness, fuck any obstacles that might lay ahead.

Finally, I shifted, giving her a gentle squeeze before loosening my hold. She sat up, wiping her eyes with the back of her hand, a small, shaky laugh escaping her lips. It was a sound of relief, of something breaking free.

"Thank you," she whispered, her voice hoarse from crying.

I just nodded, reaching out to tuck a strand of hair behind her ear. "Anytime."

We finally left that building, and I saw her safely across the walkway to the hotel to make sure she got checked in for a night on my tab.

I kissed her forehead before she left the front desk, and then I found my way to another hotel.

I was down bad for Jasmine, like 'take my money, my house, and my cars,' Jodeci bad and we didn't even kiss.

7

JASMINE
CELEBRITY LIFE BUFFET

Celebrity Life Buffet

www.celebritylifebuffet.net

Jasmine Myers wasn't playing with us. I won't hold you because our girl didn't wait one hot minute before moving on to the next.

At a recent awards show dinner, Jasmine got cozy with none other than G-Style. Yes, that "one-digit figure" G-Style. Rumor is he was eager to get Jasmine alone in a private bathroom for "conversation." Then he whisked her away from the awards show.

Jasmine, girl, if you're reading this, keep surprising us! Show the world you're not just Dylan's ex but a queen ready to be treated right. We see you, Jasmine.

-Staff Writer, We See you, Jasmine

THE FEED

MYJASMINESTAR: My name never changed, but my status did. Currently Single. Forever Fine. Peace over Pain. Me over Everything. #Single #Donewithdumb

DREALDYL: They tryin' 2 put a bro on blast but boostin' my cred. Thought she said sumthin, but I been out, been over it. Holla at me.

DREALDYL: Dropped that bag off **@MYJASMINESTAR**. I'm now free to move around the country. #Freedom #OldBagGone #Weightlimitexceeded #Waitless

GSTYLESINGS: **@DREALDYL** She's not a bag, but know I have her. CLAIMED. There is no need to speak on her ever again.

G entle. Gallant. Gracious. Good to me, G- *'Got Damn He Fine-Style* Graham Ward was everything, and the G could stand for any of those things because that man was the ultimate definition of them all. I couldn't tell up from down when he came through and gave me the pep talk of the century.

"He was the perfect place for me to land, Peyton." My words were breathy as I recalled the night before to my cousin. "He made sure that I was taken care of."

We were in the back of a town car on the way to the morning show, and I was giving her a recap of my glorious night with Graham. Nothing sexual happened, but his concern and care for me mended a piece of me right there on the spot.

Peyton looked up from her phone.

"You deserve that and more."

"He said something similar," I responded. "He made sure that I was good."

"Graham might be worth keeping around." Peyton didn't play about her endorsement of people in my life, so I made note of her recommendation. They were rare.

"Are you all planning to talk again?" she asked but returned her attention to her phone.

I shrugged. "I would like to. I'm not opposed to it, but I didn't get Graham's number."

"How did you miss that step?" Peyton admonished.

"I was in the middle of a crisis, P." I reminded her.

"Can't you DM him or something? Check his socials." She suggested.

I found that weird because she never encouraged me to contact people on social media. Either way, I still wasn't sure about what Graham and I could be. He had seen too much, seen me looking like a broken-down mess over a man who wasn't worth my time.

"After my post shutting things down with Dylan, I haven't been back on social media," I explained. "And I probably won't hop back on there for a bit. Let things settle some."

"Speaking of Dylan, let yesterday be the last communication with him, the finale. Delete his contact."

"Already done."

"I'll clean up your socials while you're interviewing today."

I nodded, thankful I didn't have to face the overwhelming responses and tags to Dylan's and my demise.

The driver let us out at the front of the radio station, and we used the elevator to ride through the building for the dreaded interview with Bizzy Brian and the Get Busy Brigade.

He hadn't changed. Brian was handsome in an offbeat way, but his personality made him unattractive. He was arrogant and braggadocious in a way he could never back up. He had been around the industry, so we knew about each other, but I tried to avoid him at all costs.

Bizzy, his associates, Peyton, and I were all settled into the room. Me, Bizzy, Big Tom, Cassidy, and Lady Lean, sat around a table with thick, soft-covered microphones mounted on it while Peyton was in the corner, out of view, doing what she did best. Brian was closest to me, wearing too much cologne and trying to be too cool.

"Q102 FM Dallas, your home for hip hop. I'm Bizzy Brian, here with the Get Busy Brigade in the studio with the baddest actress in the game, hometown hero Jasmine Myers." Brian shouted into the microphone.

"Let me scoot a little closer. If you log on to Q102fm.com, you can watch our broadcast live and see why I want to get next to her. We got a great morning mix for you, and we'll be right back to talk to the fire starter herself."

Brian pushed a button and removed the mic as Peyton hopped off her chair near the door and over to me with her tablet.

"Did you see this?" she enquired, pushing her device forward so I could see. Dylan's 'Feed' page was on the screen.

"Is he serious? A bag? He dropped me?" I looked at Peyton with disbelief, each phrase annoying more. I realized last night that I had shut down my real feelings for Dylan a long time ago. Technically, we were together, but I had checked out sometime earlier.

"But look at what G-Style wrote," Peyton smiled.

I read over the words, noticing how he responded to Dylan as if I were *his*.

"Shit," I murmured. Graham was ready to be about that action for me.

She smiled and went back to her seat.

Dylan was being a jerk, but Graham, the gentleman, was out there telling the world that I was valuable to him.

Brian pulled up 'The Feed' on his screen.

The music faded out, and Brian retook the microphone.

"I told you we had a fire starter in the building today. Jasmine Myers, ex-girlfriend/fiancée of Dylan Simons, that's right, I said *ex*, is sitting here looking as beautiful as ever." He turned to me with a wide smile. "You and Dylan were together for a while. What brought it to an end?" he threw out his first question.

"We're no different than any other couple. We grew up and grew apart. We are just at different points in our lives right now." I gave a political response.

"Well, a photo posted online says it was his fault," Brian stated.

I gave my studio laugh, no dimples, no snorts, but I didn't say anything.

"I saw that pic, man. I looked at her profile." Cassidy piped in with a shake of his head. "No disrespect, Jasmine, but looking at you in person today... Dylan was dumb to let you slip away."

"Agreed." Big Tom added. "I like a woman with a big ol' fluffy biscuit, not a pancake. Like that scene in ..." He paused. *"One Night Stand,"* Cassidy chimed in with him.

"Hands up and down, the best love scene in a movie ever, Jasmine." Cassidy continued.

"I bet you were moving your hands up and down." Brian joked.

I studio-laughed with the crew. I hadn't gotten past the awkwardness of people discussing their reactions to my body.

"At least one person is happy about the breakup." Brian made a segway back to social media. "The R&B crooner, G-Style, posted some words for Dylan. How do you feel about that?"

I smiled.

"Uh oh, she's smiling y'all." Brian joked.

"I appreciate what G-Style wrote." I shrugged. "But they're just that, words."

"I think you're holding out on us," Brian narrowed his eyes, examining me like I had something to hide. "He made sure to emphasize the word *claimed.*"

"It's in all caps," Lady Lean piped in.

"Is this a public declaration?" Brian questioned. "Do you claim him?"

"G-Style?" I sputter. "I mean, he's...Who wouldn't, um. He's cool."

"Alright, you heard it here first. Jasmine thinks G-Style is 'cool.' More hot hip-hop flava is coming your way, so stay tuned."

He pushed a button and turned the microphone away.

With a shake of his head, he leaned forward in his office chair and looked me up and down.

"I'm glad you added my show to your promo tour." He winked then.

He rolled even closer and put a hand on my thigh.

I promptly popped his hand away, "Paws to yourself."

"Rejected." Lady Lean laughed.

"Get that out of here." Big Tom acted like he was blocking a basketball shot.

Cassidy hit the bomb, falling and exploding, sound effect button.

Brian popped on a smile real quick.

"John and I go way back." He laughed.

"John?" the members of the Brigade questioned in unison.

"My first name is Jonquil," I explained with a frown. "I was named after my father, John."

Lady Lean hit the microphone button.

"This is K102fm, your home for Hip Hop, Lady Lean on the mic in the studio talking to actress Jasmine Myers. She just dropped a bomb on us. For all you real Jasmine fans, we got 102 dollars for the first caller who can tell us her *real* first name. Hint: It's not Jasmine."

Lady Lean closed us off with a song as I spoke to Brian.

"Nobody told you to share that," I said, trying to keep my cool. "Did you even consider that I wanted to keep that private?"

I had spent all these years in this industry and managed to keep my name to myself—to suppress the disappointment that it held. My father had walked out of my life before I was ten years old. I hadn't seen or spoken to him since.

Brian laughed, and his hand felt hot on my back when he patted me like we were buddies.

"Are you ashamed of your name?" he goaded.

The phone lines lit up.

"No, but if I wanted everyone to know it, I would have told it." I push his hand off of me.

Brian leaned over to whisper, "Let me make up for it over dinner."

Before I could shoot holes in his dream, several things transpired. Cassidy started bouncing up and down, motioning for Brian to pick up a phone line. An employee came through and placed the cutest ever potted red rosette succulent on the table.

The employee whispered, "This is for you," before he left.

"Ya gettin' Bizzy with Brian and the Brigade, and we're kicking it with the banging beauty, Jasmine Myers. We want to talk to the fan who knows Jasmine's first name. Who is this?"

I roll my eyes and turn my head toward Peyton, lost in her device typing this or that.

"This is the one and only G-Style." The suave voice sounded throughout the headphones.

I grabbed the microphone quickly.

"The G-Style?" I asked with a lifted eyebrow.

"Grammy award-winning, former lead singer of the boy band Young Guyz, and two-time sexiest black man alive winner, G-Style?" Lady Lean spewed off a follow-up question.

Peyton dropped the tablet onto her lap and looked at me.

Graham quickly dispelled any uncertainty with a song.

"I want to meet your body, know your body, and love your body. Just give it to me." His signature deep voice was passionate, and the words swept me back to last night when I was close to him.

"Can you meet me around ten then?" Lady Lean chimed in. *"I'm looking to get claimed too."*

"So, G-Style, we're glad you called in, but do you know Jasmine's first name?" Brian shot back unenthusiastically.

"Who cares about her?" Eileen chirped. "G-Style, it's alright if you don't know. I got a prize for you anyway," she uttered without shame. "You just have to meet me at my house to claim it."

Graham let out a hearty laugh.

"Jasmine's first name is Jonquil." He answered clearly, which intrigued me. I hadn't shared that with him.

"You're right," I cleared my throat, trying to suppress my enthusiasm. "How did you know that?"

"The audition," he said.

"What audition?" Brian inserted himself before I could get any words out.

"The Young Guyz video for *Letter Love*?" I knew the exact video. How could I forget the first time I realized my 'hood fine' size 8 was not mainstream beauty? "I was about fourteen then, and you still remember that?"

"Jonquil Jasmine Myers, you leave a light wherever you go." His voice was a velvet blanket I wanted to hold close. "You didn't get the part but left with all my attention."

"You remembered after all this time." I'm sure the awe registered in my voice.

"Time's the only thing that's changed about that," Graham replied with a throaty kind of quiet laugh. "Jonquil is a type of Daffodil, a flower. I know a lot about flowers."

I felt it with tingles all over my body.

"That you do," I answered, once again wishing my body were his petals to care for.

"I couldn't miss the opportunity to talk to you." Graham slid in so smoothly. "Did you get the succulent I had delivered? Take care of her for me."

"Yes, thank you. This plant baby is so cute." I looked down at the plant and pulled the pot closer to me. I would guard our little plant baby with my life.

"Are you still in the area, G-Style?" Eileen asked. "You two were at the Film Excellence Awards show together last night. Someone posted pictures of you two looking cozy and rushing from the building into the adjoining hotel."

"Miss Jonquil Jasmine Myers is one special woman. I had to leave town for business, but I'm trying to catch up with Jasmine as soon as she permits."

"You can check her out, large and in color, on the big screen in the new movie *Brazen Renegade*, which will be in theaters two weeks from now. You're listening to Bizzy B and the Brigade; it's time for your local weather and traffic."

Brian clicked the release button, and G-Style was gone.

"That was childish," I glared at Brian, who had essentially just hung up on G-Style, who said he wanted to see me.

"What?" He shrugged. "Don't tell me you like him?" his condescending chuckle grated on my nerves. "He's a singer. He's just as bad or worse than Dylan. Don't fall for him, J. I did you a favor."

I didn't respond to Brian because I didn't know Graham. I didn't know if I could trust him or if I should like him. I knew I felt safe with him, but at one point, I felt comfortable with Dylan. I didn't want to repeat the same mistake.

8

GRAHAM

Look who suddenly has some curves in his life! G-Style, the maestro of body-shaming anthems, has found interest in a full-figured beauty. Oh, the irony! It seems Mr. "One-Digit Figure" himself has had a change of heart— or maybe just a change of scenery. Could this be the start of a new era for G-Style? Only time will tell.

We're keeping a close eye on you. Treat this full-figured goddess like the queen she is because if you even think about reverting to your old ways, an army of empowered women will knock at your door faster than you can say "size inclusivity."

Miss Thick Chick Revolutionary, Thick Thighs & Uncovering Lies

I was annoyed. Pissed. Irritated. Spinner Records CEO Sean Walton wanted to meet in a strip club. Not just any strip club, but one that was clear across the country from where Jasmine and I had connected. I love women and all the body parts associated with them. I'd put my lips on a few and licked more than my fair share. The water from a woman's well was the glistening example of manna from the heavens. I sipped, slurped, and savored that nectar, but where I didn't want pussy juice was on my lemon pepper wings.

"Excuse me, mam," I looked up from the table in the VIP lounge where Kingston and I sat.

I tapped her left butt cheek, which had been working in concert with the right one, to clap out the song lyrics in Morse code. I didn't mind that part so much. I love women, but I wondered why she had brought her talents to my table.

The woman turned around, a sly grin pulling her lips up, before she spoke, "Yes, Papi, what can I do for you?"

"Come back in about 20 minutes," I answered. "I'm trying to eat here."

She smacked her lips and sucked her teeth before she stomped away, mumbling various curses.

"Heard you don't like girls with curves anyway." She muttered.

I had nothing to prove to her, so I let it slide. I wasn't there for fun or to fight anyone's perceptions. I was strictly there for the best lemon pepper wings ever made and to attend the mandatory meeting Sean Walton, the annoying Executive of Spinner Records, requested.

The dimly lit strip club thumped with bass-heavy music, and strobe lighting made the half-naked women glow as they strutted through the room.

"I can't believe he's got me meeting him at a strip club." Frustrated was an understatement, but taking a bite from a flat wing helped a little. "I could have gone to the studio with Jasmine this morning instead of calling in. Good looking out on the intel about her being on the show. I wouldn't have known. The extra money I paid for the rush delivery for her plant was worth hearing how happy she was."

"You like her, huh?" Kingston chuckled.

I scowled, making Kingston laugh harder.

While my semi-obsession with Jasmine wasn't public knowledge, Kingston knew I'd seen all her movies, binge-watched any series she appeared in, and never turned on a game Dylan Simmons played. It wasn't hard for anyone who paid attention to know I liked the girl.

"Why the fuck are we here, man?" I barked over the music. "I hate meetings. I hate Sean. The man could get run over by an ice cream truck, and I'd just grab a Bomb Pop. He's interrupting my plans."

"Listen, Graham," Kingston leaned back in his chair. His eyes followed the up-and-down motion of a woman on a pole in front of us but a safe distance from my food. "This is the game. He calls, and we show up. The bright side is that social media likes you today due to the Jasmine effect, and your numbers are trending up."

"Yeah, but it's not just about the numbers, Kingston. It's about the music." I dropped a wing on my plate. "And if he was thinking about the numbers, why not leave me more time to pursue Jasmine, who helped my positive trends? Make it make sense."

"Making sense? That ain't always possible with Sean."

"Where is he, anyway?" I questioned. "He called me here. Jasmine's got me feeling a little inspired to write music again, and I'm stuck here waiting on him."

"Writing music?" Kingston's voice was full of surprise.

"I haven't felt that spark, that creative energy, in a long while," I admitted.

"I haven't heard it either," he added.

"Thanks for that encouragement," I shot back dryly. I knew that Kingston was only being honest, but damn. "Anyway, I woke up with words today."

I wiped my hands on a wet nap, pulled out my phone, and shuffled to the notes app.

"Read this," I said.

"Right now?" Kingston frowned and did not attempt to turn away from the dancer.

"This is a business meeting. Yes, right now."

Reluctantly, he took my phone and began to read. When his semi-scowl lightened, I knew that I had something.

"Wow. Alright. I'm feeling the words. What's the melody?"

"I'm hearing a *He Can't Love You,* Jagged Edge kind of tune," I explained, and even though it was loud in the building, I sang through some of the lines to show him how it could fit. *"Trying to ride your curves, no swerve, I got control. You and I both know it's about to be a show. You and me can go. The distance. I'm already thinking you could be my Mrs."*

"We can make that work," Kingston nodded. "We need to get some more Jasmine in your life."

Kingston was talking about the song one second, and the next, he was silent. He was following the path of a group of women bouncing bottles and booty on their way to a table. I won't lie and say I didn't pause for a second because I like women, but I wanted Jasmine.

Sean showed up a few minutes later, loud and liquored up.

"You play a helluva chess game," Sean looked at me with a slick grin. "I have to say that I wasn't expecting that."

"What the fuck is that supposed to mean?" I never assumed positive intent with his shade tree ass.

"Is that how you spoke to the old exec?" he lifted an eyebrow.

"We're not in the boardroom, Sean."

When we were younger, his vocals were never equal to mine. Hustlers and radio stations would make mixes of our songs back to back. Most people counted me as the victor. He always thought he was more intelligent than me, hopped labels a few times, and lost consistency and momentum. I chose not to step into the business side of music. I was the better artist. I'd let him have it because I got everything else, and he seemed to need *something*. Trying to control others was more his lane than mine.

"Yeah." His eyes followed the bouncing bubble of a dancer's ass as she danced out to the floor with drinks lifted in the air. He returned his gaze to me. "I wasn't expecting you to actually *fuck* with a fat girl. It helps with the press, but you didn't have to go that far."

"You think I did that shit for my rep?" I shook my head. "How many times have you seen me do something for the label and my image only? That's not how I rock."

He shrugged, obviously no longer interested in what I had to say. "Whatever. It's a good look for sales."

"Is that why you summoned me for this little brothel adventure?" I looked between Kingston and Sean. "For some shit you could have said in a text."

He hooked a woman strolling by around the waist, pulling her onto his lap, never looking my way.

"I brought you here because I needed a plausible reason to escape. My wife, Krichelle, won't question me when I mention your name." He lifted one hand and said, "Bird, Krichelle." He used his other hand to point to me when he said, "Bird, you," then placed a hand on his chest and smugly stated, "And I'm the stone. Two birds, one stone. Problem solved."

Kingston didn't have to say, "Let's go," for me to get up. If I stayed, I would have caught a case.

I wanted to beat his ass for being a bitch, for playing with my time, and even more for talking slick about Jasmine. She was innocent. Instead of knocking his teeth in, I stood to leave.

Kingston stood, too.

Sean stayed seated, his attention on his newfound friend.

I had made it a few steps when he called my name.

"Graham?" Sean yelled haphazardly.

"Just play along," Kingston pleaded.

I turned to face him.

"Say thank you," Sean smirked.

Nostrils flaring, I let my hand clench into a fist and flatten as I prompted him to hurry up. "Say what you gotta say."

"Alright, chubby chaser," he laughed. "Instead of Chubby Checkers, we can call you Chubby Chaser since you like chubby women."

"Ask your wife, Krichelle, about what I like." I reminded him that I had shots to shoot, too. I chose to stay out of his way. I chose peace, and he better be wary of the day that I chose violence.

"Time out, boys." Kingston stepped in front of me but pressed his arm back to block any advance. "Relax. Sean, just tell us what it is you want?"

"Call Jasmine. Get her in your video. We'll cover the cost. I sent you her contact information."

He was approving the video. I would have an opportunity to have Jasmine close again if she agreed. I won this round, technically, but I still wanted to beat his ass.

9

JASMINE

Unattached. Alone. That's how I came into the world. That's how I walked into my home for the first time in my adult life. The alone part wouldn't change any time soon. I wasn't waiting, hoping, or looking over my shoulder for Dylan to appear and be my great love. I wasn't searching for signs that staying was the right decision. I wasn't ignoring the chronic churn of insecurity accompanying life with him.

I could see, like when the steam evaporated from the bathroom mirror - it was clear. There had never been a more accurate statement in my life than 'When you know, you know.' I knew. I didn't have to see either of the men to understand what I felt in my core. Dylan was the past, and Graham would hopefully be a part of my present.

I walked into my bedroom without turning on the light. I was exhausted and just wanted to sleep.

I fell into the bed without looking and nearly jumped out of my skin when the covers flopped over and scrunched down.

"You think that dancing muthafucka really like you?" his voice startled me. Even in the husky whisper, I could hear the anger.

"Dylan, what the hell?" I yelped, instantly on edge. The nerve of him. "What are you doing here?"

"I stay here." He barked. "Or did you forget you got a good man at home while you were out playing with captain lame?"

I clicked on the bedside lamp and illuminated half of his face. I couldn't find the irresistible charm that once had me hooked.

His eyes were the same. His handsome face hadn't changed. Those thick, full lips were a game-changer whenever he wielded them, but my feelings had changed, and my eyes wouldn't let my body be excited about him anymore.

"Get out." The words came out in a low grumble.

"You're out of line right now," he scoffed. "You're in public at a hotel with another man, but telling *me* to get out? Whatever happened to never cheating or disrespecting me?" His voice grew louder with each word.

"Let's not even start on body counts," I yelled.

"Fuck that. You're mine. We've been in this and are about to ride in this." He pointed toward the bed. "You think we just stop here? I bought you these sheets and made that pussy wet up all of them."

"Take the damn sheets," I screamed, hopping out of the bed, pulling each corner up and off the bed while he lay in them. "Take these ugly sheets and your community dick and get out of my house!"

He could get mad, throw a tantrum, or pout, but it wouldn't change how I felt or what I knew—we were through.

"You're tripping." He hollered, rolling over as I actively tried to pull him and the sheets off. "You gonna be real salty when you gotta put these sheets back on."

"You need to leave, *now*."

"And have more of these bloggers talking shit? Is that what you want? You say I'm bad for your image, but you're running the streets with that washed-up fake Usher Raymond. That's better? He's better than me?"

I didn't answer; I went straight for the closet. I was **done**. I gathered Dylan's things, pulling his clothing from the hangers and onto the floor.

"What the fuck are you doing?" He worked at putting things back. His anger flared to life when I tossed his sneaker collection at his face.

"You almost hit me," he ducked.

"Get out, Dylan," I gritted. My actions faster, my voice thudding with each shoe. "Take all your shit and get out of my house!"

"You think basketball players get girls?" He snarled while dodging his random items. "Them singing muthafuckas get pussy plated and served to them. You couldn't handle the shit with me; he's about to turn your whole life upside down and and leave you face down for dead."

His face transformed into something terrible, something I never imagined would fall between us - hate. Dylan continued to tear into me.

"You're too emotional, Jas - always have been. That's why I needed to be with someone else. You were smothering me. I couldn't blink my own damn eyes without you saying it's too dark."

"Get out." I wouldn't go back and forth with him about that. I wouldn't debate my worth with him.

"Final answer?" His gaze was intense as he watched my eyes.

"Final fucking answer." And I meant every word.

There were a few seconds when he glared and waited, and the silence stretched the chasm that had already grown between us.

"Bet." He turned and gathered a few pieces from the floor and shoved some things in a duffle bag. "But when he's done using you, don't look for me." Then he exited my home and, hopefully, my life forever.

10

GRAHAM

I was sitting in my home studio, trying to remind myself she was *just* a woman. I couldn't go out like a chump. The soft hum of equipment and a beat for an unfinished track was on loop in the background. I tapped on the desk while staring at Jasmine's phone number. I had to take the chance. Taking a deep breath, I hit the call button and listened to the ringtone, my heart pounding like a bass drum.

"Hello?" Her sultry voice filtered through the phone and straight to my groin. Everything about her turned me on.

"Hey, Jasmine," I greeted calmly, even though I was juking and jigging on the inside. "It's Graham. How are you? Is this a good time for you to talk?"

"Wow, two pop-up calls. I might start to think you like me." Her tone was a mix of surprise and amusement. "To what do I owe this unexpected pleasure?"

"I've been thinking about you since awards night."

I could hear the smile in her words. "I bet you say that to all the girls."

"Nah, I mean it." I leaned back in my chair, trying to act cool, but my nerves were jumping like grasshoppers. "You've got this glow, Jasmine. Can't fake that."

"Ok, cheesy," she teased, but the words warmed me like we shared an inside joke. "But I do appreciate the compliment."

"No cap, no cheese, just real talk," I said, a grin spreading. "Actually, I'm calling because I need a favor. "

"Let's hear it," she replied.

"I've got a video shoot coming up in Atlanta," I began, and I could feel my heart thumping in my chest. "It's for a new track, and I've been racking my brain trying to find the perfect person to be in it. Then I thought, who better than Jasmine?"

She was silent for a while, and I could almost see her raised eyebrow. "You want me in your video?" she asked, her tone somewhere between flattered and incredulous. "You didn't even choose me for your video when we were teenagers. Remember? Cute girl number two? You picked someone else."

I ran a hand over my face. My dumbass groupmates and that crazy director couldn't see what I saw and the beauty that millions of people adore on their television and big screen.

"Yeah, I remember. My bad on that. But look, I'm trying to make up for it. You game?"

"Hmm," she paused. "You know, I might have to make you work for it."

"Please believe I know how to put in that work." And I meant that. All she had to do was say *yes*. I hadn't even thought of anyone else to be in the video.

"I firmly believe in *showing* me, but don't tell me." She responded playfully.

"You gotta get here, and I got you."

"Oh, yeah?" She was all in. She knew it, and I knew it, but I didn't mind letting her draw it out.

"With one hundred percent certainty, come see me, and I got you. All expenses paid, appearance fee, hotel, spending money. I put that on my mama's flowers."

"Not her flowers," she sounded amused, and I was glad. "Is the video all that this trip is about?"

I was ready for her question because I was ready for her.

"Jasmine, no bull shit. I'm trying to handle this business and see if we can discover some pleasure together." I had no way to finesse it, so I had to be honest. I wanted her for the video and me. "We'll shoot the video that day and hang out that night somewhere other than a bathroom. You can think of it as a taste and see."

"A taste and see?" she questioned, her tone light. "Um, what's on the menu?"

"I meant, come get a taste of life with me and see how long you want to stay. The choice is yours."

I didn't realize that I was holding my breath until she gave the best answer I could have imagined, and I released it with a sigh.

"I'm intrigued by the thought of getting a taste of you, so I'm in." She agreed.

"You won't regret it," I promised. "I'll have my team send you the details. And Jasmine?"

"Yeah?"

"Thanks. This means a lot to me."

"Don't thank me yet," she warned playfully. "I might just outshine you on camera and steal the spotlight."

I laughed again, feeling a rush of anticipation. "You don't have to steal what's already yours."

We said our goodbyes, and I hung up, my heart still racing. I could feel it in my bones. Jasmine was more than just a face from the past; she was a force and having her in my video would change everything.

11

JASMINE

I had made it to the Atlanta soundstage for Graham's video shoot and was impressed. The staff was very nice and attentive without being in my face, the director was kind, and I had my own trailer for wardrobe, hair, and makeup. Upon arrival, Graham wasn't around but made sure I felt special. As I entered my trailer, potted plants and leaf clippings in clear bulbs were on a table for me.

Peyton had picked up the card when she placed her bag down, finding the note before I even had the sense to look because I was in awe. Growth and beauty surrounded me.

"On my mama's flowers, I got you." Peyton read aloud slowly while trying to assess their meaning. "P.S. These are actual plants and clippings from my mama's house. She was excited to share when she learned you're my video girl."

She looked at me, confused when she asked, "What is this about?"

I was already rolling over with laughter, so it was hard to talk. When I finally explained the meaning behind the card, it only made Peyton say, "Oh," even though it had completely warmed my heart and other parts.

The director wasn't as well known as Kema but had a good

following and was easy to work with. One-on-one, we viewed lines and walked through a storyboard to understand the premise. Basically, it was a romantic date scenario with Graham singing to me.

Standing on the soundstage after hair, makeup, and wardrobe, looking at the director, I had to make sure that I didn't hear voices. I searched the faces of the people surrounding us in the room. They were waiting.

Sit on his lap? I thought I heard the director, a thin man in short pants and a long shirt, say that he wanted me to straddle Graham. Did I want to? Yes. There wasn't a being on this earth that I wanted to 'bend it low and spread it wide' for Graham Ward more than me, but there were so many people on set.

"Did you say that you want me to straddle him?" I took a few steps closer, squinted, and slightly turned my head to the side, hoping it might help me decipher the directions better.

"Yes." His red glasses slid down his nose as he bent to look into the camera. "The song is about G-Style knowing a woman's body and her giving it to him."

I nodded because I understood the song and sentiment.

"It should be sensual." The director stood and rolled his arms like waves. "You should flow into each other like you want to consume each other."

I moved in front of Graham, watching how he stared me down. He was on the set bed in a white T-shirt and black joggers. It was a decent-sized soundstage. People were in chairs and standing around. The director looked severe, with one arm folded against his chest and the other hand beneath his chin, trading glances between a screen and the live set.

"That's going to look amazing," he said. "I want the angles perfect."

He walked over to another camera set up on a tripod. They were shooting multiple angles simultaneously to get the most footage. The scenes would be edited together later without doing a thousand retakes.

The first shot, the first scene that the director wanted to film, was me sliding a leg over Graham's lap and lowering down his body. I wasn't sure what I signed up for, but I was so glad I did.

Graham stood. His lean, muscled body taunted me with each step. The grin playing on his lips made me want to play with myself and him or play with myself *for* him.

"You alright?" Graham asked quietly. He wasn't touching me, but I could feel him everywhere. He was close.

I had done love scenes before. I understood the art of illusion, but this was G-Style. I didn't have to make-believe. I didn't have to pretend for him. I wanted Graham.

He took one of my hands in his. He was still wearing that grin, the one that put me at ease and made my libido spin.

"Did you add this to the script?" I narrowed my eyes at him.

"What makes you think that?"

"It wasn't in the original blocking of the scene, but it does benefit you."

"Come on now, Gem. You know me better than that. If I wanted to bust a move," he tore his gaze away from mine to look over my shoulder and around the room before returning his eyes to mine, "I wouldn't have done it in front of all these people. You'd at least have to buy me dinner first."

"I did want to visit That Place With Pancakes." I chuckled. I needed to shake off the nerves, so I took a deep breath. "Is it too late to blow this joint and get a meal?"

"Seriously..." G said, "this was all a production decision. I wasn't included. If you're uncomfortable, say the word, and I'll have them switch it up."

He rested a hand on my folded elbow, instantly soothing me. I made the mistake of looking at where his large hand connected our bodies and then up into his glinting eyes. They caught the shine from the stage lights perfectly. If mesmerized were a person, she'd be me.

I had already trusted him with my mess, tears, and tragic love, and I trusted him to take care of me on the set, too. Everything felt natural with him.

"For the movies, they have an intimacy coach, someone who choreographs the scene, and then we just follow the steps," I explained. "What we're doing is freestyle, maybe even a little real, and…" I hesitated, letting my eyes drift over the expanse of the set. The wardrobe team, makeup, set crew, light crew, directors, agents, friends, publicists, and random people were all there waiting and watching.

"Oh, you're shy?" he asked, re-examining the space as well.

"I'm not shy, but it's different with *you*." I couldn't look at him then. I felt childish. I had a crush. It was just a crush, and it was hard to fake what was real. I couldn't let that keep me from doing my job.

"How about this?" Graham started, taking both of my hands. "I'll have some people clear out, and then we move like no one is here."

I leaned forward and lifted my face toward his ear, my pebbled nipples grazing the front of his shirt, as I whispered, "And what if I cum?"

A deep hum rumbled from his throat like he could taste my sensation, which satisfied his soul.

The way he hooked my waist and, with quiet force, had me ready to take him to the trailer.

"You about to get this production shut down if you keep playing," he rumbled.

I wasn't playing. Being around Graham made all the horny I had stored up march into my pussy at once, demanding to be released on his dick.

"I don't want to embarrass myself," I whispered.

"You won't. The first place that you get to cum for me is on my tongue, and if you ready for that, I need to end this play shit and get our night started."

He stepped back before saying, "It's on you." With a nod toward the bed on set and then to the door marked Exit, he asked, "We rocking or are we rolling? Either one, I can handle."

I had to keep on my big girl panties—for now. I let my hands flop, shaking my torso and reserves away, loosening up before I turned to the director and gave him a thumbs up.

"Alright. Cameras are set. Frame's ready," the director said, looking at the mini viewing screen in front of him. "Jasmine, just as we rehearsed, but with the addition of sitting on Graham for the sensual shot."

"Got it." I nodded.

As if I hadn't acknowledged that I understood, the director stepped over to walk and talk through the shot. Again. I wanted to finish it, but I had to be patient.

"Start in the vanity and pretend to finish your makeup for a night out. G-Style will touch you, trying to coax you to dance." He did a stiff wiggle when he said the word *dance* as an example before he continued. "You give in, and a sexy dance grind takes place. There's a dip. Stand up, move stage right, and Jasmine, you dance alone in the background as G sings to the camera, sits, then leans back on the bed."

I nod. The director made it seem so technical. He literally did a squat when he mentioned the word *dip* and took giant steps while describing our forward movement.

"And don't forget to find your way across to his lap before the end of the chorus." When the director turned his head, Graham lifted his arms in defense.

"Chill. We don't need a demonstration of that."

"Ok." The director clapped his hands as he laughed and moved off the set. "Let's go."

"You ready?" Graham asked. "Say the word, and I'll air this place out."

I could tell he was serious and that my comfort was his priority.

"I'm ready."

Taking my position I stood in the mirror and picked up the lipstick.

"And, action." The director shouted.

I began smoothing the lipstick across my lips, playing it up for the camera and puckering loudly.

"You look good in that dress, baby," Graham complimented as he walked behind me.

I ignored him and popped my lips a few times.

I felt his warm hands on my waist. Cue the migration of a million tingles across my skin.

"Dance with me." He swayed.

Graham draped his body across my back and placed his hands firmly on the dresser and vanity.

"G-Style, you're going to make me mess up my makeup," I say, bumping my butt against him. "You're not even dressed."

"I'm trying to put you on."

He moved back playfully, acting like my little bump pushed him back across the room.

If we were a couple in real life, he would never have to worry about that, and I would never push him away.

"Why are you holding out on me?" He nearly growled the last word into my ear, his lips tracing the shell, as he slid a hand up the side of my hip to perch an arm on my hips. That felt damn good. It was like he found a new part of my body to enjoy every time we did the scene.

I wanted to yell cut and keep going at the same time because he wasn't playing fair.

"Cue music," the director instructed.

The opening chords of his song filled the soundstage so that we could keep time with the lyrics. The editing team would dub over it later for the final product.

G-Style took the lipstick and threw it behind him, and then he pulled my body into his. I melted into the warmth of his hard body.

"You know I can't resist you," he uttered, but I couldn't tell if he meant it for the sake of the video or if he meant it.

"We're going to be late." I batted at his arm.

He held me even tighter and nuzzled against my neck.

"Just a dance. That's it," I said, pretending to give in.

The beat of the music changed, and Graham began to sing. He was made for music. Something about his voice caused my senses to liquefy and leave my body.

"I want to love you from the inside out, with my body and my heart, head to toe. Let me show you what real love's about," he sang.

Our grinding bodies collided forward, rolled back, and moved left and right simultaneously. I took advantage of touching Graham as we moved.

His mouth swept softly across the skin of my neck.

I felt his every word, heartbeat, and movement like we were linked - in tune. His hips moved the words, and his hands told me he meant every last one. He would get to know my body, inside and out, very soon.

"You know you want it, and I'm going to give it to you. Feel it; you don't have to steal it. You know I'm going to give it to you." He sang.

I had never been so emotionally connected when acting. I knew how to separate truth and fiction, the real from the fake, but the lines did more than blur with Graham. They disappeared.

G-Style gave me a spin, then dipped me across his knee as the song continued.

I stood up and stepped away but left my breath with him. I watched in awe as he moved to the bed to sit, singing passionate words I wanted to receive.

I moved to the back of the room and began swaying my hips again from side to side, raising my arms in the air. Then, I made my way to the front of the set.

Graham looked up at me as I slid down onto his lap.

He winked when I was seated because I felt all of him pressed against my core, feeling the vibrations of him singing as I pressed my breast into his forearm.

I felt the trail of his fingers slide down my back in time with the melody, gripping my ass like he'd thought about it a few times, drawing me closer.

I rock forward, bowing my back dramatically as I circle my hips against his lap. He was hard against me, and I was a soft mess drifting off into a dream world wrapped in him, soothed by his voice, and amped by his presence. I throbbed for him. My eyes closed because I didn't need to see, just feel. Circle, press, neck roll, back bow, chest rub, enjoy, repeat. I couldn't hear the music anymore. All I could hear was Graham over the beat of my core pounding.

"Cut," the director yelled, breaking through my haze.

I was about to remove myself from Graham, one toe on the ground when he clutched my leg back in place.

He didn't say a word, just stood up with me still attached to him and moved us through the set as though I were weightless. I hadn't opened my eyes. Graham picked me up like I was groceries. No struggle whatsoever, and that shit turned me on. I kept my legs crossed at his back, and he kept me secure. Stable, no huff and puff or jerky movements, he had me.

"Amazing job. The next few scenes are short and cute." The director's voice faded as he called to his star. "Graham? G-Style! Hey, where are you going?"

I buried my face into the warm smell of spicy amber and ginger wafting from Graham and didn't ask any questions. I was going with it, with him, wherever he wanted to take me.

I heard several doors open and shut before we stopped, and he placed me on a hard surface.

I released him, letting my feet fall and bounce against cabinets. He had taken me to his trailer and placed me on the counter of the small kitchenette.

As I lifted my head, Graham lowered his, our foreheads meeting in the middle.

"Damn." He breathed against my cheek. "You got my dick ready to drill through these pants."

"How can I help?" I asked. I was open to anything. I was open *to him*.

12

GRAHAM

Her lips tasted like a peach mango smoothie. I had been fighting my attraction to her since she walked through the soundstage door. Holding her in my arms, feeling her body against mine, and knowing she was willing to invite me into her world made her irresistible. Having her that close to me, calling her mine, even if it were fake, built an urgent need in me that wouldn't be fulfilled unless I tasted her, just a little.

In my trailer, I had her on my counter, set up like the best meal, and I was a starving man. It was messed up that I couldn't indulge. Work. I also couldn't work with a boulder between my legs.

I could barely ask for a kiss before she had her soft lips pressed against mine. Full, juicy, confident lips that connected without caution. I thought we would be compatible. I imagined that when our mouths met, I would enjoy the tangling of our tongues, but I was wrong. The insatiable need that tore through me when our tongues collided had me clamping onto her ass to stay tethered. I needed the connection to keep me from floating away. There were noises - smacking, slurping, sucking. It wasn't a pretty kiss, not quiet or compliant. Our kiss was raw and teasing, a race to release what had been brewing between us.

I cupped her breasts, my heart racing as I kneaded the plump circle and thumbed at her thick, taut nipples.

Her hands moved across my back and abs, around my neck, and across my head. She couldn't be still, and I couldn't move her close enough.

"Damn," I leaned back, gasping for air.

She rested her head against the wall, panting words between gulps of air, "I don't think that solved the problem."

I kissed her cheek before popping her thigh, taking a moment to make butterfly pecks across the skin of her inviting neck.

"Nah. That was exactly it," I corrected. "That was motivation to get through this day, to see what I can get into tonight."

"Cheesy, cheese ball." She laughed.

"You like that shit." I nipped her chin lightly.

"And do." Jasmine agreed, pushing forward and sliding down in front of me. "Tonight is a definite must, and I plan to hear all the cheese and corn chip lines you sing in your songs."

The graze of her body against mine caused a punch of want to spur in my gut.

"It ain't corny if it's true, Gem." For that, I looked her in the eye. I needed her to know that the compliments and come-ons were genuine. "I don't care if it's cheesy... I like you."

"We should probably get back to set." She ignored my bit of truth. "Don't want this to drag out too long."

"Alright. Play me to the left, but you'll figure out I'm right for you soon enough."

She smiled, even though she said, "Come on, Frito's. Let's go."

After I willed my arousal to go down with thoughts of a zombie apocalypse, the video shoot went by quickly enough. There were only two wardrobe changes for both of us, and most of the scenes were in the interior bedroom set and in front of a green screen.

Hours later, Jasmine rode back to the hotel with me in the chauffeured car. We had arrived for the shoot at different times due to prior scheduled events, but the rest of the night was ours together.

I had my two normal guards with me. We entered through the back to avoid the people hanging around the front of the hotel, but I still used my body to shield her as we entered.

"There are three rooms on this floor," I explained as we exited the elevator.

She looked between the doors as though she were confused.

"I have my own room?"

"You're always welcome in my room." I grinned. "I didn't want to assume anything about tonight."

"I appreciate that." She reached up, leaning forward to kiss my cheek. "Where are you taking me for dinner?"

"It's a surprise," I answered.

"You said that in the car."

"I meant that in the car."

"I meant it when I said that I don't like surprises. I need to look up the menu. I need to plan my wardrobe based on the level and theme of the establishment. You've witnessed what can happen with me and certain foods. I don't want to clash with the decor. There are reasons that I need to know where we're going."

"There are reasons that I don't want to tell you." I wrapped an arm around her waist and placed a hand at her back, drawing her closer. "I understand what you're saying but trust me. I can handle any food or clothing-related emergencies. Dress casual. I've informed them you're allergic to citrus and asked for our privacy."

"That was very thoughtful of you. I'll trust you. I'll be out in about an hour."

I stood still, watching as she turned and sashayed the space of the hall to her room, and I regretted trying to be the gentleman with every jiggle of her ass.

"Aight. One hour." I repeated.

She was ready within an hour and walked out of her room in a flowing dress, looking like she was about to walk through gardens in paradise, and her presence would bless the flowers.

The car ride was short but seemed to take forever because I was anxious about her reaction. I had promised a lot for the reservation.

The cafe was quaint. Wrought iron tables and chairs with colorful cushions made the outside of That Place With Pancakes look like they belonged on a movie set. Long wisteria tree branches swayed across large clear windows, and fairy lights on wooden pergolas made the place look magical.

"No!" she breathed the word against the window before swiveling her head back to me. "You didn't."

"See, isn't it better as a surprise?"

"No." She swallowed her smile before I could enjoy it.

"Don't be like that." I kissed the corner of her mouth.

"How did you know that this is my favorite place in the whole wide world?" She was giddy. "I've wanted to visit the original location for years but never had time, or they couldn't accommodate my reservation."

"Now you have time, and I got us a reservation," I responded as the car stopped. I tapped the driver to stay seated, so I exited the car and opened the door for my date.

Truthfully, I hadn't known it was her favorite place, but when she mentioned it on set, I had my people work on getting us in.

"How did you even get a reservation? This location is the smallest and the only one in the country with a month-long waiting list."

"I'm G-Style, baby. It's what I do." I chuckled.

"Thank you," she said, sliding out of the SUV in front of me. Her eyes swept up and over my face with gratitude as she spoke. "This was very thoughtful."

"Thinking of you has been happening a lot lately."

She felt good against me. Her in my arms was addictive.

We entered the restaurant, a nod to the nostalgic diner. Crisscrossing beams lined the ceiling, and the smell of fried sweet batter filled the air.

"Mr. Graham, Ms. Jasmine, right this way," a young woman with a twangy accent greeted us. She spoke and walked as fast as she smiled, leading us to the biggest booth in the back corner. "I'm Claire. We've been expecting you since you called today in a rush and needed to get a reservation. We appreciate you coming to this location. The staff is so excited that you agreed to take pictures with everyone after your meal. We told the few customers not to bother you, too."

"You're telling all my business, Claire. I was trying to impress her." I smiled so that the waitress knew that I was joking.

"I apologize, Mr. Graham. I'm always running my mouth. Pretend you never heard that, Ms. Jasmine."

"It's all good." I dismissed. "My goal is to keep a smile on this lady's face. So far, you're doing a great job."

Jasmine narrowed her eyes at me as we sat, and the waitress flitted away.

"You promised to take pictures with the entire staff to get this reservation?"

"Yes. The entire damn staff." I growsed.

"You hate taking pictures with fans," she acknowledged.

"It's a minor inconvenience for a major reward."

Jasmine's face was painted an array of emotions, eyes bright with curiosity and caution, and chin lifted with determination. She was still guarded, but I could see a twitch of a smile at the edge of her lips.

"You don't have to be hard, Gem. Just let us be."

Claire took our drink and food orders because Jasmine already knew what she wanted, and I doubled hers.

Jasmine wasted no time getting to the center of her uncertainty.

"Why am I here, Graham?" she asked, folding her arms across her chest. I hoped to let those breasts rest in my palms soon.

"I'm assuming your mama thought your daddy was kind of fly. The two got together - badda boom, badda bing," I joke.

Jasmine picked up a sugar packet and chunked it at me.

"Why did you want me in your video now? Especially since you don't like big girls."

"That bullshit again." I was sick of people acting like one line in one song was my truth. "It was a song."

"*You* sang the song," she asserted, and even though I could tell she was a little annoyed, I was glad she felt comfortable expressing herself. "It's also a pattern. I've never seen you with a girl over a certain size."

"So you've seen everybody that I've dated, huh?" I tried to keep the irritation out of my voice, but I was tired of the conversation. I liked Jasmine, and her doubting that made me want to grind my teeth.

"You know what I mean," she smacked her lips, and her little head tilt was cute. "None of the women you dated publicly were thick."

"You saw me with girls who wanted to be seen. Maybe I wanted someone special for myself. I signed up to be in the spotlight. Who I choose to date shouldn't have to be. The internet isn't a safe place for some women. I don't need people picking apart and tearing down my girl. You know better than anyone how sharing your partner can backfire."

"True," she sighed.

"And evil didn't start with the internet," I leaned forward, putting her hand in mine. I needed her to understand my sincerity. "When I was a kid, my mom had a lot of problems with women being terrible to her because she was overweight."

"Your dad was in the NFL, right?" Jasmine asked before taking a sip of water.

I nodded.

"And my mom was a model," I added. "She gained weight when she had me, then she got sick, and the medication made her put on weight. She didn't look like the model that she was before. She didn't look like the other football wives. They were relentless in the way that they talked about her. She eventually stopped going to events and just stayed in the house. Flowers didn't compare and criticize, so she focused on interior design and floral arrangements. When she wasn't in the world, she was her happiest. She found beauty on her own terms, but because people were so ugly to her, she kept a close circle."

Jasmine rubbed her thumb in a circle around my wrist.

"That kind of negativity can make anyone retreat," she empathized, her voice soothing and encouraging me to continue sharing.

"I know the chaos that comes with my lifestyle. I'm not setting anyone up for failure. I'm not ashamed of the women I date, but I know what this world is capable of and what I would do if they came for someone I cared about."

Jasmine didn't say anything, just nodded. Maybe she needed time to take in the words and understand my intent. Being popular had its perks, but it also had drawbacks. Any woman I dated seriously would be scrutinized. Jasmine had already been through so much. I wanted her, but I also wanted to see her succeed. I wasn't sure what that would look like.

Claire was back with a smiling face while balancing plates on a tray. She noticed our joined hands and placed the plates accordingly.

"Thank you," Jasmine smiled at the woman.

"You're more than welcome." She looked between us, grinning like she held a winning lottery ticket. "I just want to say I'm so happy for you two."

"Appreciate it. Give us about 30 minutes."

"Right. Sure," Claire sputtered as if just remembering she was staring at us. The waitress hurried away and I turned my attention to Jasmine.

Jasmine never let go of my hand, and I loved the feel of her skin beneath my fingertips and enjoyed touching her.

"I've dated women of every size. Keeping my love life private wasn't about shame. It was about privacy and protection. How can I nurture a bond that everyone is trying to destroy? It was about shielding someone that I cared about from the spotlight. I hope one day I can be your protection, too."

Reluctantly, I let go of her hand so that we could eat.

"Hearing your why makes me feel better," Jasmine said as she cut through her pancakes. "You talk about your mom a lot; she must have had a big influence on your life."

After chewing and swallowing, I answered.

"She was there." I shrugged and took in a small bit of bacon. "My dad was on the road with the team but was absent whenever he did come home. We never connected. He saw that I was into art and music and didn't know what to do with that. I spent more time with my mom, uncle, and grandma. When I turned thirteen, I was off on the road with the Young Guyz and then my solo projects."

I waited until she finished her juice before I asked her a question.

"Since you're throwing out the hard questions, why did you stay with Dylan, especially after what he did to you publicly?"

"My therapist says that I accept less than I am worth because I like to maintain a connection and avoid the pain of abandonment." Her answer was plain like she was describing mayonnaise.

"What would you say?" I asked, pulling her fingers into mine.

"I didn't give up on people because they messed up," she shrugged. "I used to believe that even if people I loved hurt me, cutting them out of my life was wrong. As long as they tried to make changes, it was okay. I stayed because I believed. I hoped. I adjusted. I'm not some helpless doormat that he walked all over." She placed her fork down before continuing. "You have to understand that I thought that I was being loyal. I thought I had realistic standards and that all rich men cheat."

"That's not true."

"I believe differently now." She quickly added. "Dylan didn't hit me, and he gave me money. Some days were enjoyable. It was easier to deal with the devil that I knew than to jump out there and try something different. I knew what I was getting with him. No surprises."

"Are you and Dylan over?"

"Completely." She nodded. "I deserve better."

"Let me reintroduce myself," I said, placing my fork on the table and reaching out to shake her hand. "Hello, my name is Better."

13

JASMINE

All of the gentleness Graham had held onto was let loose. We barely made it through the door before clothing flew in multiple directions. We were in his suite, but there was no time to look at the walls and decor. I was actively trying to get him housed between my walls. It was a private space for us where only we could be.

The kiss was hectic, our mouths were crashing together in a need to be joined and only separated for breathing purposes.

I took advantage of touching him everywhere, releasing all of the feelings careening through me.

When he stepped back, separating us, I wanted to leap onto his waist and attach myself. I fought the urge only to see what he had in mind for me.

We stood, face to face, in various stages of undress, panting, waiting, and wanting. I wouldn't rush because I had already waited what seemed like forever, and I had no certainty that forever would allow this man to stroll that big dick my way again. I would enjoy the night.

"When you dreamed of me, what did you think about?" He asked.

I licked my lips but kept quiet as I let my eyes fall on the thick imprint straining at his core.

"Tell me."

I wanted whatever reward he would give me for following directions, so I gave him the quick and dirty of my most recurring teen fantasies of him.

"I thought of you while I fucked my fingers. I thought of you watching me cum all over my hand for you. I thought of you getting so turned on that you had to stroke your dick."

"Oh yeah?" His voice was low, and his hand was already near his crotch.

"Mmhm," I nodded while touching my nipple, enjoying watching the evidence of him liking my words making his pants tent.

"Tell me more."

"My gushy pussy, made you hard as steel." I wasn't sure where my shirt had landed, but it was gone, and I pressed down the cups of my bra so that my tiddies spilled out for him. "I love a hard dick."

"Do you?" he asked, stepping out of his pants. His shirt was missing, too, and the sight of his tight boxer briefs only made me wetter.

"Yep." I popped my lips on the end of the word because they wanted to pop on him.

He leaned down to latch onto my right nipple then, and I found it more difficult to stand, but the more I talked, the more he touched - so I said words.

"You stroked yourself to climax for me and then poured all that creamy nut onto my belly." I huffed out. "And as your prize, you got to lick all the juices between my thighs."

Graham flattened his tongue around my areola, the graze of his tongue setting off waves of desire before he stood straight and backed away.

"Get on the bed. Show me how wet that pussy gets," Graham winked. "I'm trying to win my prize."

In life in general, I did not run. I did not jog. But for Graham, I scurried my big ass across that room to that bed so fast I could have broken a world-wide record.

"Take them panties off," he ordered.

I did.

"Show me," Graham demanded.

I did. I let my knees fall apart, angling my feet outward so Graham could see my center clearly.

"Fucking perfection." He commented, the words dripping with want as he clenched his fist open and shut.

"You need something to do with your hands?" It wasn't a question, more of an observation. "Show me yours. Use your hands and give me a show to cum to."

I propped the pillows up behind me to see all of him unobstructed.

He got rid of the last piece, hiding that bold shaft. The way it bobbed out, bouncing forward to stand up proud and brown, I felt it needed a damn theme song. He was long and wide, and that sledgehammer looked ready to knock down my walls.

"Touch it." He spoke. His eyes were pinned directly on me.

I eased two fingers into myself and lifted my hips toward my palm while imagining how good Graham would feel.

I reveled in watching him gather and release his dick while he enjoyed the sight of me. I pressed with more vigor, humming with delight.

It was the dirty grin for me. It was the way he choked his dick like he would handle me that confidently too.

The pulse around my fingers drove my rhythm, and I rocked into my hand, brushing my clit against the base.

"Keep doing that," he groaned. "So damn sexy."

I wanted him to feel good by seeing me.

"I hear you, baby. She's drenched." He commented, and I began to throb.

"Stroke it faster," I demanded, and he did, kneading into his length over and over.

That sight—him standing there, flat-footed, shoulders squared, head straight, and eyes focused on me like I was the superstar, his star—made me feel like I was floating above the stars.

We looked at each other, pleasing ourselves as we primed our bodies for the experience.

"Graham," I called out to him as I released all over my hand.

"Yea, baby," he groaned before standing right over me and setting his nut free. "Jasmine."

More satisfying was watching him drip all that goodness onto my stomach's skin. Bold. Legs spread apart, one large hand gripping the length of his shaft while the other graced the base, strong neck strained, head lifted to the heavens, he looked glorious. If there was a moment that I wished to have for life, it was him standing above me at the height of ecstasy, his body on full display, finding me so irresistible that he erupted.

He fell onto the bed, and his breathing was a rush of spurts as he took in gulps of air.

"I didn't forget about my prize." He said breathlessly. "One minute."

I chuckled at that but quickly changed my tune a few seconds later.

I lost track of life as he lowered himself to lick me clean, not leaving a drop. I squirmed and shivered until my world shattered into pieces, and then he pulled me back together again in his arms.

"I could hold you like this forever if you let me," he whispered in my ear. We were already attached.

14

JASMINE

It's Maddie Show

"Turn your volume up and come a little closer because you know you want to hear this tea. Now, y'all know I've been watching this G-Style and Jasmine Myers situation unfold, and I gotta say, it's got me scratching my head and wanting to gag at the same time.

First of all, can we talk about how Jasmine suddenly popped up on the set of G-Style's new video as the vixen? Girl, what?!

And then, there was that whole scene at the restaurant, That Place With Pancakes, where G-Style, who usually avoids cameras like they're a bad ex, was all smiles taking pictures with the staff. Come on now. When did he become Mr. Sociable? Somebody's PR team is working overtime to make us believe he likes her, and honey, they are working hard!

Why would G-Style, Mr. One-Digit Figure, suddenly go for a full-figured woman like Jasmine? And Jasmine, sweetheart, are you going along with it because Dylan's got a new woman knocked up? Yep. That dirty dog, Dylan, has a new baby mama.

Dylan done had a whole other baby on her. After all these years, she can't keep that man tied down, but you expect us to believe she could snatch up G-Style? Not likely. Sell it to somebody else.

I bet Jasmine is using G-Style as a cover to keep her from looking lonely and pathetic out in these streets. The drama is juicy, and we're here for every minute of it! Where there's smoke, there's fire, and I love to watch it burn!"

Maddie's Minute Monologue, It's Maddie Show
-Madison Humphries

Madison Humphries made me understand why people risked jail time for acting on homicidal thoughts. I had marched back and forth in a straight line more than a newbie at an HBCU band camp. I was trying to work through my nerves, but every time I thought about how she'd made it her mission to embarrass and exploit my pain, I got pissed all over again. My life was toxic entertainment, yet again.

"I loathe that woman," I yelled, stopping to put my hands on my hip and tap my house shoe against the hotel's soft carpeted floor. "Why the fuck is she worried about who my cooch wants to say 'hi' to?"

"What exactly are you mad about?" he asked, obviously not as pressed about the situation as I was.

"Did you not hear Madison say we're faking this whole thing?" I vexed, not understanding why he wasn't pacing the floor with me.

He shrugged. "I also heard Madison say that Dylan has a new baby mama. You could be mad about that."

"Why would I be mad about Dylan?" I stopped pacing to ask him, because what? Who cared about Dylan? Not me.

"You just answered my question with a question, so I don't know what has you in your feelings over there." Graham expressed with more volume than I was used to. Was he hurt? I couldn't tell if he was jealous and couldn't understand why he would be. After what we shared, he must have thought I could sit in his presence and be upset about another man - as if his aura didn't eclipse every thought of any other man I'd known.

"The answer is never Dylan. Nothing about him adds up except his body count and child support payments. He's someone else's problem now." I had no more energy for Dylan and the daycare center he was trying to populate. The stinging hurt wasn't there. The sadness didn't snatch at my throat or push tears out of my eyes. I didn't feel trapped by his foolishness because I was no longer a part of it.

I resumed pacing, annoyed at Madison and annoyed that Graham thought I had feelings left for Dylan.

"What I don't like is how she came for our..." I didn't know what to call it. What were we? "How could she insinuate that you wouldn't want to be with me?"

"Come here," Graham said. He was calm, and the deep tenor of his voice did something to me. It left my body no choice but to comply.

I wanted to be angry but felt he would make that difficult. Pouting and dragging my feet, I moved toward his open arms. It was becoming my new favorite destination. I fit perfectly between his legs and leaned back to relax my back against his chest.

"I wonder if you're upset because she touched on the truth?" he asked. "What are we doing?"

It was hard to think while he rubbed his hands across my shoulders and over my arms.

"We have a mutually beneficial situation," I answered.

"A situation?" He purposefully kept his voice flat. I could tell that he was trying to remain neutral, but he still sounded like he might be a little offended.

"I like you. You like me." I explained.

"You sound like a Barney song," he said. "Be real with me. Are we building something?"

"This is good. This is private." I winced as I turned to face him, folding my legs under my bottom.

"You can talk to me, Gem. Tell me what's swimming around in that head of yours." Graham pressed a loose curl behind my ear.

"I'm enjoying slow and loose," I admitted. "I don't know what this could be, but my focus is my career."

He nodded. "I understand that."

"Does that change this?" I moved my finger between us. "Can this be something that we do for now?"

"Your answer just lets me know where my heart should go," he answered. "I won't dust him off just yet."

"We could go wrong, really fast, and publicly," I remind him. "Another high-profile relationship gone wrong is a big risk."

He leaned forward, taking my mouth with his and pulling my body forward so that our chests met, and I understood how right he was. I understood that trying to give him up wouldn't be easy.

"Come away with me this weekend," he asked when he let go of my lips. "I have a friend with a Yacht and staff we could take advantage of for a day or two."

"Me going away with you doesn't change that it'll look like we're trying too hard. As Madison said, if we're seen together too much, it will look like a promotional stunt."

"No pictures, no people, and no one will bother us in the ocean." He added. "We can go as fast or slow as you need as long as we go together."

Being away for a few days with Graham sounded like the softest place to land. I wasn't opposed to being with him; I was opposed to the media circus that surrounded us.

"How do we do this without the media intruding?" I asked.

"No one matters but me and you, but if someone got something to say, I have no problem handling up." He emphasized.

I had seen Graham's former versions of handling the media over the years—hands over lenses, curse words, direct responses in comment sections, or fist to jaw for those who went too far. While I hated that we had to address media concerns, it was nice to have a partner who was there to address them with me. It was refreshing to feel like I wasn't trying to figure it out alone.

"Let's keep it as low-key as possible," I suggested.

"Alright. If we're going incog-negro, let's enter separately, low hats and glasses. No posts, no notices to your industry people about your location." He added. "I'm here for whatever makes you feel comfortable."

"So this is real?" I say out loud, more to convince myself than as a question. "We're going to spend the weekend together?"

He took my bottom lip into his teeth before he answered, "We're going to spend the weekend together."

"That's good because I need more of this," I said, parting his lips with mine and letting our tongues meet again.

Graham was the first to come up for air.

"Now that we have that all worked out, I have a favor to ask."

"What is that?"

"We have a few days before our schedules get crazy. This weekend, I don't want half of you. Don't give me a little bit. I want it *all*. I want you to be free with me, free from judgment, frustration, irritation, and reservations—just me, you, and 48 hours free of inhibitions, and I promise you, no doubt, this is worth it."

I agreed wholeheartedly.

15

JASMINE

We talked about politics. We talked about our families. We talked about books. We even talked about sex and not one time did I feel unsure or suspicious about what he said. Our conversation flowed, and Graham was open and honest. It was freeing to speak my mind and know my words wouldn't be purposely misunderstood. It was freeing to listen to him, measure his words against reality, and see that everything lined up like a haircut. I knew deep down that this wasn't temporary. It wasn't about the childhood crush or me being a size sixteen. It was about mutual admiration and respect.

We carefully boarded the yacht, making sure to disguise ourselves and arrive at different times. Graham stayed below deck until we got far away from the dock. All staff had to sign a Non-Disclosure Agreement, promising not to reveal any information about us or our trip without risking a lawsuit and financial penalty.

He was masterfully created, body, face, and mind, and I was in awe of him. I felt blessed to be close to him—touch, feel, kiss, and enjoy him—with free and unlimited access. The beautiful part of the scenario was that Graham was just as fascinated with me.

He was laid across a sofa on the sundeck - face up to the sun, eyes closed, chest gleaming, large hands at his side, abs popping, and legs bubbled with muscle. He was the picture of bliss.

"Thank you," I exhaled breathlessly. I was blessed. Graham was a blessing, and I took the opportunity to watch him sleep to admire him fully.

After a few seconds of perusing, I heard his sleepy, husky voice.

"Do it," he said, maintaining his calm demeanor. His eyes didn't open. His body didn't flinch.

"Do what?" I questioned.

"Whatever it is you're overthinking," he said evenly, as though he already knew me. "You're staring like you want to do something to me. Come do it."

He sat up then, eyes open and intense on me. I had the urge to break out in a full Friday night revival kind of shout because the experience of Graham up close deserves a palms-to-the-sky two-step.

"Quit acting like this ain't what you want," he added. "I'm down for whatever your mind is cooking over there."

I moved toward Graham on the sofa near the railing.

With Dylan, I had to be cautious. He was testy often. I had to catch him in the right mood, and even then, he still might snap at me. He might push me away, feigning body aches, some miscellaneous action that upset him, or annoyance from a random thing I said.

Graham rose to his full height, moving with majestic steps to meet me.

He caught my eyes with his and slid his fingers into the waistband of my shorts.

"I didn't want to bother you if you were resting," I admit. "I didn't want to be clingy."

"As long as I have a body, you can make yourself at home." He dipped his head down to my lips, pecking them softly. "Cling to me, Gem. I'm here with you. I'm here *for* you."

I didn't know what to say to that.

"What did I ask of you before we left?" Graham asked.

"No inhibitions."

"I'm going to move like you're already mine, and I expect the same." He chided and clarified simultaneously as he popped my ass. "Come over here."

Graham led us back to his chill spot.

"Why are you playing nice when it comes to something you want? I am what you want, right?"

"Damn right," I said too loud and with too much enthusiasm.

I didn't think Graham had any insecurities, but he wondered if my liking matched his. I didn't want him to have any doubts.

"Why the hesitation?" he whispered against my neck before peppering kisses across my collarbone.

"I was taught that good girls don't want sex," I explained. Even though I knew it wasn't true, those were the parameters set out for me as a kid. "Good girls, wait. They don't take the lead with sex."

He slipped his hand down the front of my shorts.

"Who said you were a good girl?" he asked, and I whimpered when he landed at my center. "When you're hungry and people are playing with your time and food, what do you do?"

"Tell them to give me my damn food," I groaned.

He leaned in closer, placing his face beside mine, "What do you want, J? Tell me what you need."

I inhaled the soft salt water smell mixed in with his spicy cologne and rubbed my cheek lightly against the stubble on his face.

"Tell me." He hummed.

Quickly, I found the place that had taken control of my thoughts. "Give me my dick."

"Gladly." He growled before producing a condom from his swim shorts pocket. "Bend over."

My shorts had disappeared. I felt him moving my swimsuit over to the side and his finger pressed at my entrance.

"Already so wet for me," Graham commented.

"I want it," I moaned while leaning back against him.

He tunneled into me, grabbing onto my hips as he pressed forward.

"More," I called out to him because the dick felt like it had been supercharged by the sun.

I bucked back as he crashed against me with a plunge so deep and firm I felt him everywhere. A fury of tingles invaded me with collision.

"More," I moaned, and he gave me his all.

I held onto the couch like it was my lifeline, the one thing keeping me tethered to this earth as his dick actively tried to take me from this existence. I loved every second of pouncing against his tight thighs and the plow of his fat-brimmed dick against my walls.

"My Gem," Graham grunted as he increased the pace. "Your pussy is priceless."

"Then take her, Mr. Beast," I yelped while working against his rhythm. Each powerful thrust cracked away more of my reserve. We started with my face down and ass up, my only view was the brightly colored seat covers, but with each slam of our bodies together, I rose. My head lifted, my shoulders climbed, and my chest felt the sun as I took him all in.

Delight lit across my body as whatever restraint Graham had crumbled as well. He pulled me back against him, cupping my breasts as I clamped my body to his. He drilled into me so enthusiastically that our friction could have lit a fire if he hadn't made a soppy mess.

It didn't take long before his grunts turned to growls. He bit against my shoulder, muffling his roar as I felt him tremble and release.

My core pulsed, and I milked him for all that he would give me, stretching out the explosion of bliss that had taken over all of my senses.

We fell against the sofa, still connected, languid, and spent.

16

JASMINE

I didn't know my soul was searching for peace until I found it and felt it with *him*. The realization wasn't jarring. It didn't shake me or make me fall to my feet. It was as gentle and stable as our movement through the water. It flooded me soundlessly, making its presence known. The anxiousness had been washed away. The worry had been cleared as though it was never there. The clock on the wall ticked, and all I could do was tingle in the places where he licked. My body wouldn't let me do anything besides lay in his arms, cocooned in his warmth, with his hard length pressed against me. Leaving the space where he kept me had no appeal whatsoever.

One arm wrapped around my waist, the other splayed across the pillow, his hand in front of me. I couldn't help but trace the veiny protrusions on his brown skin. For the first time, I noticed a small tattoo, a thin line of intricate musical notes.

Reaching for my phone, I angled it so that even though Graham was extremely close, his face wasn't seen, but his wrist was. I moved my head and snapped a few poses, my hair on his arm and the tattoo. My phone was connected to the boat's Wi-Fi, so I sent the pictures to Peyton with one text:

"Peace."

"I like that," Graham said as he rubbed my thigh.

"You just play possum all of the time, huh?"

"I'm a light sleeper," Graham chuckled as he pecked my cheek and exited the bed.

I watched him disappear into the restroom and reappear a few minutes later.

"You hungry?" Graham asked as he moved toward the door.

"You cooking?" I smirked. Something about being with him made me feel like being playful.

"Is that an answer?"

"Do you need an answer?"

"You gonna cook with me?"

"Do you want me to cook with you?"

"Answer a question, woman," he rushed to the bed, sliding against the sheets to pull me into him. I couldn't hold in my laughter anymore.

Graham commenced kissing me all over my neck, nuzzling his fuzzy face against my skin, and I couldn't stop giggling.

"Yes." I cackled.

"Yes, to what?" he asked between kisses.

"Yes. To. Everything." I croaked between words.

"That's what I thought."

He was on his feet in a few swift movements, and I was over his shoulder.

"Graham! Wait! Woah!" I half howled and half giggled. "Don't drop me."

He had a firm grip on my thighs. He had me placed securely against him, but still. I couldn't remember a time when a man had carried me. I felt weightless. I felt cared for. I felt wanted. And I needed all of those feelings.

Placing me on the kitchen counter, Graham was between my legs, looking at me like he wanted to make me his meal, and I was eating every second of it.

His eyes flickered with warmth, and I was comfortable in our silent exchange of admiration.

"Thank you for taking this chance with me," he said between kisses.

My stomach spoke to Graham in the language of hunger, making a loud, grumbly sound.

"Guess we better make this food then," he laughed, pecked my lips, and helped me off the counter.

Together, we moved around the galley, grabbing utensils and food like a team, even though we didn't know exactly where everything was. We laughed as we helped each other navigate the space, and I was delighted that I'd joined.

We ate in the dining area near the floor-to-ceiling windows showcasing the water. Staff had set the table with fresh flowers, plates, and utensils. The first few minutes were silent as we ate until Graham asked a question.

"I remember you saying you lived with your aunt and Peyton. How did that come about?" Graham took a bite of his food as he waited for my response.

I didn't talk about that much. It wasn't that I couldn't. I just didn't. It was complex. On the one hand, I grew up with my cousin in a family member's home, who treated me decently. On the other hand, the woman who gave birth to me gave up on her role in my life.

"My mom was always working," I answered without much emotion. "I have an older brother who hustled and wasn't around much. It was me and her, but mostly me. She worked evenings and overnights, so she wasn't home much when I was there. I walked to and from school, made my meals, did what she asked, and tried not to need anything."

Graham listened quietly, occasionally moving his fork to eat or taking my wrist in his hand with a soothing thumb across.

I took a bite of my pancake, needing something sweet, before I continued explaining.

"My mom's brother, Uncle Christian, found out I was home alone a lot. His wife, Aunt Sharon, started picking me up from school to help out. I'm the same age as their daughter, Peyton. I kept Peyton busy while my aunt went to her social clubs. I was more mature and more worldly than Peyton needed to be, so I looked out for her. At first, my aunt felt it would be easier if I went to the same school as Peyton. After we went to the same school, she felt I should stay with them during the week. Over time, I stopped going home on the weekends. My mom wasn't concerned. She just kept living. She looked relieved, mostly when I left, and annoyed when I showed up. She never visited me, and I stopped going to visit her. We're cordial still, but the same rules apply - I don't bother her, and she doesn't bother me."

Graham traced a line across my wrist. His gentle touch instantly soothed my fraying nerves.

"My aunt was in one of her social groups when they asked her if I could be a model for a flyer," I explained, recalling how my career started. "She was so flattered that I was chosen. Another woman in the group was connected to a modeling agency. The next thing I know, I'm doing commercials and bit roles, auditioning for music video appearances - that I didn't get."

I shot Graham a playful glare. I wasn't upset about that. Things worked out as they should have.

"That wasn't my fault," he reminded me. "I wanted you to be in the video."

"So you say." I teased. I knew he liked me then.

"What about your dad? Aren't you named after him?"

"My dad's exit was less dramatic," I explained. "He left before I was double digits. He went to work one day and never showed up again. My mom eventually told me that he got tired of being an adult, found him a gullible girlfriend to live off of, and avoided a real job so he didn't have to pay child support. I like my first name, but he doesn't deserve the honor of using it for a career I built."

"Did your mom show up once you got famous and started making money?" Graham asked.

"My aunt was not for the back and forth. You're in or out, and my mother was out."

"How involved is your aunt now? It seems like Peyton handles things primarily."

"Peyton keeps me together. My aunt and I parted ways once I got deep with Dylan. He was bad for my image, bad for me. She wanted me to distance myself from him, but I wouldn't listen. I wanted something of my own, a decision no one else had a part in. I wanted him and was tired of my aunt dictating my life. Peyton had been around soaking up the knowledge and went to college for entertainment management. She took over the title."

"Do you regret it?"

"Firing my aunt? No. Dylan? Not anymore." I gave the most simple answer to an overcomplicated issue. "I learned some things, and I'm grateful for where I am now."

Graham smiled at that before taking my hand and guiding me over to his lap. "I'm grateful for where you are right now, too."

17

GRAHAM

I'd felt good pussy before. I'd had plenty of opportunities over the years to indulge, and I was a glutton. I enjoyed the hell out of those women, but when I fell into Jasmine - and I mean it felt like her pussy cradled my dick and guided me through a bottomless pleasure tunnel - I knew that I was *home*. She took all of me with so much ease that even my fucking hair follicles were shocked and amazed. I think my hair grew when I entered her. My whole body was electric, from eyebrows to toenail tips. I felt like I had plugged into a high voltage supertwat, and my life would never be the same.

She was it for me. The beginning of love and the ending of my drifting dick days.

I woke up with a song in my heart. The words came to me, floated through my mind, and I listened to the melody of her soft breaths. I couldn't sleep. The lyrics pressed to escape. The need to express how much I cared for her was urgent.

"It's in your smile - go crazy when I haven't seen it in a while. It's in your touch. I can never get too much. Don't want to be without it - so glad I found it. We're new, but there's no doubt about it. I want to be with you - only with you. I just want you."

"That's beautiful."

Her voice startled me. I was expecting her to still be asleep. I hadn't written music in years, and it was scary to have someone hear it, especially the person that the song was written for.

"Better than cheesy corn chips?"

"No cheese, no corn." She smiled through the words as she moved closer to bend down and place a quick kiss on my lips. "It reminds me of your earlier work, the real G-Style."

"Why do you say that? It wasn't even a whole verse."

"The wording, the vibe - so many things."

"Tell me more." I turned my body toward hers. As usual, the soft beauty of her natural face in the early morning light was breathtaking. I was amazed by the creation that was her.

"It has the feel of your first solo album, which is my favorite. That one song." She snapped her fingers before she spoke through the words. *"The words were like - I saw you once, now I can't get you outta my mind. Dreamin' 'bout the day you'll be mine, you're a rare find. You're so fine, but it wasn't the right time."*

I chuckled at her talk-singing the words.

"I wrote that song about a girl I connected with from a distance and didn't take the chance to get to know when I should have."

"She must have made an impression on you."

"Yeah." I caught her eyes, wondering if she caught on to the fact that *she* was the girl. She was the girl I wanted but was cuffed to someone else before I could build up the nerve.

"The stuff that you sing now doesn't have the same soul. It's observational but like in a critique of women. It's less personal."

"You noticed all of that?"

"It was so obvious to me," Jasmine said through a frown. "Was there something that made you shift?"

"I lost my inspiration, to be honest." I shrugged. "They wanted everything. The record label pushed me to produce music faster and tour longer. I pushed through so many opportunities that would have made finding a genuine inspiration easier."

"You didn't write the songs on the last two projects." She gasped.

"That's not common knowledge," I shook my head as I explained. "They brought in ghostwriters and found old songs from other artists. I didn't write anything about *Perfect Girl*."

"Damn. That's the song that led to all the trouble."

"The song that led me to the *perfect girl* in *real* life." I corrected.

"It makes sense," she noted, glossing over my declaration. "Your early music felt like a love letter to love. Lately, these songs have been trendy and surface. They've been missing depth and soul."

"Tell me how you feel." I winced. Even though it wasn't my writing, it still hurt to hear her negative opinion.

"I like what you sang earlier. Run it back for me."

I smiled at her use of terminology and assertiveness.

"You heard me." She nodded toward the keyboard. "Let me hear it."

"You got it, boss."

I cleared my throat and twinkled out the song's first few chords.

"It's in your smile - go crazy when I haven't seen it in a while. It's in your touch. I can never get too much. Don't want to be without it - so glad I found it. We're new, but there's no doubt about it. I want to be with you - only with you. I just want you."

I lazily continued the chord progression, playing with some notes, when the unexpected happened.

At first, her voice was a soft soprano, but it bloomed into a rich, textured alto as she picked up the song where I left off with her own words.

"It's in your voice, the way you say the words, that let me know. There's no stop; it's all go. You already got it; you won't have to be without it. It's new, but I want you. I want to be, have to be with you. With you, only with you."

I kept playing, hoping she would add more. Her voice was so authentic and effortless.

"You never told me you could sing," I said before ending the tune.

"A little bit." She gave a bashful grin.

"I've never been serenaded."

"I don't sing for just anybody. It's not something I do in front of anyone, but your song inspired me."

"Sing for me again." I kissed her cheek.

"I was just playing around."

I kissed her lips before asking again. "Sing to me."

Jasmine didn't sing but moaned when I pushed my hand between her thighs to press against her warm and wet center.

"Damn, baby," I nearly sang myself. She felt amazing. "Give me my song."

"With you." She sang the two words like a summoning siren, and I gleefully fell against her as I butterfly kissed across her collarbone.

"Only you." She called out.

18

GRAHAM

www.Celebritylifebuffet.net

I'm calling Jasmine and G to the red carpet because did they just dip out on the world for a Caribbean vacation? An amateur drone operator flew a device to film aerial water views but filmed way more than was expected. The best way to find out your ex-fiancé has a baby on the way is on a yacht taking deep stroke backshots from your new boo. We love to see it. I won't hold you. I thought there would never be a day when Jasmine stepped away from Dylan. If anyone could break a spell, it would be G-Style. I don't know if I should cheer or shed a tear that it took so long for her to find him. Either way, our girl is free, and we love the look, but is this just a one-time thing? Is G-Style ready to settle down? Jasmine just broke free. Is she ready to be cuffed?

Staff Writer, Look Who Found Freedom

THE FEED

DREALDYL: Don't fall off the boat with that reach. Couple where? Those screenshots were made on the internet. AI at its best. He doesn't like her. #fake

GSTYLESINGS: @DREALDYL Don't be a hater all of your life. Those who can't just hate.

DREALDYL: @GSTYLESINGS Never thought you did leftovers.

GSTYLESINGS: @DREALDYL Nah, she left, and it's over for you. It's good eating where I'm sitting. #openbuffet

DREALDYL: @MYJASMINESTAR know how I do. She'll be right where I left her when I'm ready for her. #Stats and #Status #CaughtFish

GSTYLESINGS: @DREALDYL Do what you do, but don't speak on mine. No thumb wars. Pull up. #notimeforfakeones

B eing with Jasmine was different. Time flew by when we snuck off together and crept slowly between our meetings. There was no other source for how she felt. The only thing that I wanted was to be laid up somewhere with my girl. We hadn't made anything official, but I was determined.

I missed holding her. I missed her giggle snort. I missed her flat singing notes and bright smile. I missed our connection. She had press for her movie and I had preparations for the album release and the Freedom Awards honor I was receiving. We were two busy people with full lives, but she had found ways to share a little of herself daily. Shared social media posts, 'good morning' texts, and a random call when time permitted helped to soothe some of the stabbing need to be near her.

As soon as I walked through the door, I knew it was a bad idea. Sean Walton had texted me, requesting I meet him at a random restaurant without Kingston. There was something wrong. The place was beautiful. Water fountains, flower walls, strategic lighting, and jazzy music created a refreshing vibe.

Then I saw her - Krichelle Walton. She stood, and I knew why she was standing there, but I didn't understand what would make her want to meet me in private after so many years.

"Hi, Graham," Krichelle spoke, leaning in for a church hug.

"Hey," I answered before asking a question. "Where's Sean?"

"Let's sit and order drinks before I tell you why we're here."

Her response had bullshit written all over it, but the server showed up quickly, we ordered drinks, and I waited.

"I know you're surprised, but I couldn't find any other way to get answers."

"Answers to what exactly?" I had an idea but needed her to confirm.

"Why didn't you ever bring me into the light? I was always your dirty little secret." She paused when the server was back with our drink order. "People thought I worked for you, and you never let me share the truth."

I didn't deny what she said. I was young when Krichelle and I dated. She did studio work and sang background vocals back then. She was also not skinny or the type that other male artists were seen around town with.

"Why her? We were good together. I was bigger then, sure, but I've always been beautiful. I slimmed down, eventually."

Krichelle had put in the hard work to get the appearance that she wanted.

"The problem wasn't your appearance, Krichelle. I was young. I didn't know how to navigate a relationship. I was caught up in ego and what others would think."

"I wanted to marry you. I loved you." She confessed.

"I apologize for hurting you. Back then, we were just learning to love ourselves. I had no clue how to love you. I thought that I was protecting our relationship by keeping it under wraps. I thought it was good that no one knew, and you could be free from the scrutiny of women who wanted to be in your spot."

Krichelle bit her lip as she looked at the table.

"I wanted us to work," Krichelle said, her voice filled with resignation.

"Your brother didn't." I reminded her. Bizzy Brian had been a thorn in my side since Krichelle and I met. Brian had gotten his popular radio and podcast show after I left Krichelle, but he refused to play any of my music. He never outed my relationship with his sister, but he said he disliked how I moved.

"Brian is Brian, and no one can change that." She took a sip from her glass before continuing. "It was weird seeing the pictures of you smiling down at her, kissing her, and she's about the same size that I was back then. You looked so content. I've never seen that on you before."

"I like Jasmine," I admit.

"I can tell."

"You eventually found Sean." I reminded Krichelle. She had married Sean Walton a year after she and I split. While I assumed he wanted to be with Krichelle because she had been mine, no one knew. From what I could tell, the two had a genuine connection.

"He was never you," she admitted. "I'm leaving him, and I thought maybe...since I look different... since you're not serious..."

"I *am* serious about Jasmine." The words felt right. They were the truth. I cared deeply about Jasmine. The ugly part, I wouldn't say out loud, was that I had never felt as deeply for her. We were cool, but there was a reason beyond my immaturity that we couldn't take it to the next level.

"I understand, and I'm not happy for you, but I wish you happiness... if that makes sense." She said, dawning a fake smile.

The server returned to take our order.

She didn't mention our past or future again, and we spent the next hour catching up on significant events and mutual acquaintances.

She apologized for the false pretense, thanked me for my honesty, and ended the night with a quick hug goodbye.

19

JASMINE

Brian was beyond annoying, and if his radio station hadn't been sponsoring a screening of my movie *"Brazen Renegade,"* I would have happily dismissed him. Instead, we were in a secluded room at a movie theater, preparing to surprise the audience.

I hoped to keep ignoring him, but he couldn't let that happen either.

Brian stepped over with his phone outstretched.

"Look at this," he said.

When I didn't immediately give him my attention, he said, "Didn't I tell you?"

I swiveled my neck toward him and let my eyes follow.

"Tell me what?" I sighed. I didn't want to talk to him, and I would have gladly gone if there were any other locations where I could wait without him.

"Graham." He practically spat out the name. "Asshole used to date my sister and is now trying to get back with her."

I looked at his phone closely, then recognized the faces—Graham, looking all fine and lickable, hugging Krichelle Walton, a willowy woman with long, straight hair and a flat nose.

I lifted my eyes to Brian and asked, "Is Krichelle your sister?"

"He didn't tell you?" He seemed to find pleasure in his statement.

"We don't talk about you or her," I added.

"Graham and Chelle were together for years. It's messed up that he's still hiding their relationship." He shook his head. "I'm not mad because Chelle upgraded from the help to the CEO, but Graham played her, and I don't want to see that happen to you."

What Brian said wasn't news to me. While Graham and I hadn't spoken about Krichelle being related to Brian, Graham called last night to inform me about their orchestrated meeting. He explained their entire lopsided love triangle to prepare me for any news stories that could arise. The event was about to begin, so I wasn't interested in a conversation with Brian.

"I don't know what happened between them," I said after an exhale. "Graham has been straightforward with me and about me."

I had no doubt in my mind that if I wanted to go public, Graham would write our names in the sky in front of the New York Times building. The hug didn't concern me. I had seen passion flare in his eyes, memorized the row of his brow and lift of his lip when he growled out his ecstasy. That look, the one he was giving Krichelle in the picture, looked like cousins leaving the cookout. What bothered me was that another person I was dating had me looking stupid in the world.

"He never claimed my sister publicly because of her size." Brian asserted.

"Krichelle is thin," I reminded him because I was a little confused. I had seen her a few times over the years at events. "She's exactly the one-digit figure G sang about."

"She wasn't skinny back then," Brian laughed. "It took a few surgeries, a nutritionist, a chef, and a fitness trainer to get the Krichelle you've seen. Sean paid for it all. Graham had her carrying garment bags and equipment when they went out so she'd look like an employee instead of helping her. Krichelle was too good for him then, and you're too good for him now. I'm telling you this because I care."

"You can keep your care. I didn't ask for it. This is about revenge." I scoffed, moving closer because the amount of restraint I needed to keep from cursing him out kept my voice low. "For every single time you laughed on air about how Dylan treated me or clowned me for staying with him, it could have been a phone call to see if I was alright. Instead, you ridiculed me and acted like Dylan was right because he was rich. If you cared, you would have treated me like a human being with feelings instead of a hot topic."

His face twisted up like something stank, and the little bit of handsome he had faded away.

"You should be hopping on this dick in gratitude that I got him exposed. Where's your pride?" He popped one hand against the other, clapping with each point. "I gave you all the proof that G-Style is a user, but *I'm* the one not treating you like a human? I still haven't seen him publicly claim you. He had your ass out on a boat but can't call you his woman to a blogger? Sounds disrespectful to me."

"What's disrespectful is you gossiping like a teenager," I shot back. "What's devastating is that no one likes you. The only way to feel good about yourself is to find the flaws in others. Find a mirror, and next time you think you care about me, don't..."

Before I could finish the last word, the promoter was there, ready to escort us to the front. I had to use all my acting skills and replay a memory of Graham between my thighs to dredge up the energy to excite the crowd.

I was pissed about Brian, but I also knew Graham. I trusted Graham. Trusting Graham was a relief.

20

JASMINE

The kitchen was filled with the warm, comforting smell of cornmeal and sizzling oil. Peyton stood beside me, expertly mixing the ingredients for Aunt Sharon's famous hot water cornbread. The sun filtered through the window, casting a golden hue over the room, and I felt a sense of peace. It was as if the chaos of the past few months had finally started to settle, and I was finding my footing again.

"Okay, Jazzy, you're up," Peyton handed me the wooden spoon. "Time to get your hands dirty."

I stared at the bowl of yellow cornmeal, water, and salt in front of me. Aunt Sharon's hot water cornbread was a family legend, but I had never actually learned how to make it. I loved my aunt from a distance and embraced the family that didn't make me feel small or unworthy. No matter how much I wanted the recipe, I wasn't calling her for it, so I enlisted Peyton.

"Alright, let's do this," I said before taking the spoon and stirring the mixture. The warm water made the cornmeal feel smooth and almost soothing against my fingers.

Peyton watched me nodding in approval as I mixed. "Not bad,

not bad. Now, remember, it's all in the wrist. You want to get the right consistency."

I followed her instructions, focusing on getting the texture just right. As we worked, Peyton leaned back against the counter, her eyes softening as she watched me.

"I'm so glad to see this," Peyton commented.

"What? You're glad to see me cooking?" I questioned.

"You being curious. You're finally doing something outside of worrying about Dylan and the blogs. It's been ages since we cooked together," she said, her voice gentle. "You've seemed a lot happier lately. More like yourself."

I glanced up at my cousin.

"Really?" I wondered if it had been that obvious how stressed I was all the time with Dylan. My world revolved around him. "I mean, I guess I feel better, more grounded."

Peyton nodded, a knowing smile playing on her lips. "It shows. Since you've spent time with Graham, you're glowing, girl."

Being with Graham was just that—moments filled with comfort and relaxation. We just vibed. Beyond the fact that he sometimes put syrup on his eggs and didn't eat peanut butter anything, we fit. It was easy. We both had the same spiritual foundation, similar outlooks on spending and career focus. I liked him.

I felt a smile trying to pop out, and I wanted to hide it by focusing on the cornmeal.

"Graham's been... good for me. I feel like I can finally be myself with someone. He isn't critical or harsh. It's refreshing."

I released the smile that I had been trying to hide.

"The first time I saw him," I reminisced out loud, "I felt *all* the things."

"All the things?" Peyton questioned.

"All. The. Things." I reiterated.

Peyton's smile widened. "I'm glad to hear that. And I have a little confession to make."

I looked up, curiosity piqued. "Oh? What's that?"

"Well, remember how you always liked Graham? I discovered he'd always had a crush on you, too. One of his backup dancers gets her hair braided at the same shop as me and says he kept a pinup of your *One Night Stand* on his tour bus." She paused, a mischievous glint in her eyes. "He's a good guy, so I kind of... helped push things a bit."

I blinked, processing her words. "Pushed? What do you mean?"

Peyton chuckled, leaning in conspiratorially. "I had a little chat with Kingston, Graham's manager. We thought you two would be perfect for each other. So, we might have nudged things along. We made sure both of you were at the Film Excellence Awards."

I stared at her, a mix of shock and amusement. "You what?"

"Come on, Jazzy! You needed a push, and I knew Graham was into you. He's a good guy, and you deserve someone who appreciates you. So I played a bit of matchmaker."

I couldn't help but laugh, shaking my head in disbelief. "I can't believe you did that. But thank you, Peyton. I guess it worked out, huh?"

Peyton shrugged, a satisfied smile on her face. "I knew it would. I didn't send fifty reminders to Dylan, but he played his part as an inattentive boyfriend perfectly. Sometimes, we all need a little help finding the right person. And look at you now, making hot water cornbread and falling in love. It's a beautiful thing."

I felt warmth spreading through me, not just from the hot water in the bowl but also from realizing that I was finally finding my happiness. I looked at Peyton, gratitude filling my heart.

"Thank you, Peyton," I saluted, my voice soft. "For everything. For believing in me and for setting this whole thing up."

Then, the unfathomable occurred. Peyton leaned forward and wrapped me in a hug. She didn't show affection often, and I relished this rare show.

"Anytime." She whispered. "You're my cousin and my best friend. I just want to see you happy."

That's when the joyful tears I had been trying to hold on to pressed out of my eyes.

"You deserved better than Dylan," Peyton continued. "You deserved better than to be fired from a movie for being human. And I'm glad you didn't give up on Graham."

"Me too." I sniffled. "Thank you for loving me."

The people in my world were not perfect, but I was grateful for those who provided a safe place to be myself. I held them close.

"It's easy to let fear and doubt control your life after what you've been through," Peyton added. "You're stronger than that."

I clung to her, tears trailing my face, and released the last of my apprehension. No blogger or talk show host could take anything away from me that wasn't meant to be mine. My place in this world and the love I received from those who mattered didn't hinge on public opinion.

"I am."

Peyton pulled back, looking me in the eyes. "You're more than a survivor. And you have people who believe in you. Don't let the others bring you down."

I smiled, feeling a sense of contentment that had been missing for so long. I was no longer the girl who felt lost and unsure of herself. I was finding my way, one step at a time.

The doorbell rang, interrupting my thoughts. I looked over to Peyton.

"Who could that be?" I asked.

"Not sure." Peyton lifted her shoulders near her ears and dropped them in an extra dramatic shrug. She was a horrible liar. I learned that the hard way when we were kids. Aunt Sharon only had to ask Peyton once, who sloshed all of her fingernail polish across a cardboard box to make a painting. She could have won a Grammy for singing my name and an Oscar for how she cried. "I'll finish this last piece while you answer the door."

My slides flopped against the hardwood floors as I walked to the door. From the hallway video panel, the screen showed that Kema Bridges was standing on my doorstep.

Confused, I opened the door to let her in.

"Hey, girl," she greeted, leaning in for our customary pat on the shoulder that mimicked a hug. "Peyton invited me over."

"I figured," I said with a lifted eyebrow. "Come on back here. We're in the kitchen."

Kema shifted a satchel on her shoulder as she smiled and walked behind me.

"Are these new scripts?" I asked, looking back at the woman. Realization dawned as I slid down from my emotional high into everyday life. "That's why you're here, right?"

Excitement squashed out the lingering sadness as I thought about what kind of role would bring Kema to my front door. A new role was always inspiring. Being someone else, somewhere else, used to help me forget the pain associated with my real life. I didn't feel the urge to run away from life this time. The day-to-day with Graham made me want to stay present and explore me.

I took Kema to the kitchen, and she sat in a high bar chair at the counter next to Peyton.

"I'm making my dream movie!" she squealed. The slap of the thick manuscript against the counter made me giddy.

"I'm so happy for you!" I gave Kema a real hug. She had been working on several manuscripts and dreaming about making movies since I met her on set long ago. "Which story? What studio?"

"Completely independently funded by an angel investment group, so I get to call the shots and make the film I want with the people I want."

"Amazing."

Kema's face turned serious as she slid the manuscript to me.

I pulled the story close with glee, ready to delve into the possibilities.

Flipping through the pages, I scanned the words, looking for a character that stood out.

I shot a quick look at my cousin. Peyton also enjoyed the new scripts. Scripts were new opportunities for funds and exposure, which led to more funds—making money made Peyton happy.

The slight jiggle of her foot against the bar chair told me that Peyton was excited about this script.

"You've read it already?" I asked her, but I already knew. "Tell me about it."

If Peyton couldn't be still, then it had to be good.

Interviewers often asked how I chose my roles. I never told anyone that the tap of my cousin's toes drove me to say *yes*. If the words on the page could make her react, the script had to be a winner.

"It's the first installment of a superhero series," Peyton explained. "It's about a single mother who worked as a tour guide in the Louisiana swamps. After she finds a crystal on the banks of the river, she gains super-hero powers."

Still flipping through the pages, I nod in approval of the premise.

"Is it an ensemble? Are there other superheroes in the story?"

The shake of Peyton's head stopped my hand in the middle of a page-turn.

A grin spread across my cousin's face, and I knew it was what I hoped for.

"It would be *you*, all you, Jasmine." Her eyebrow lifted as she squealed out a shriek that could summon dolphins.

"A lead role!" Jumping up from the chair, I did a quick little shuffle and shimmy.

Peyton joined me by clapping and bouncing.

"I waited to be sure it was a real possibility," Kema explained. "You would play Siyara, the lead, with a leading six-figure salary."

Placing one steadying hand against Peyton's shoulder and the other against Kema's arm, I looked up toward the ceiling, letting the beginning of tears flow from my eyes. After twenty years of photo shoots, casting calls, bit parts, and being the neck-rolling best friend or temptress, I had a quality lead role.

21

GRAHAM

It's Maddie Show

People are gonna learn to trust me. Auntie Maddie is not playing when it comes to what's happening. I know things. Now, put your listening ears on. I spoke to the CEO himself, Sean Walton, to confirm everything I already knew. He had to bribe G-Style with a big budget for a video so that he would have Jasmine in it. His relationship with Jasmine was set up in a boardroom, just like I told you. He don't want that girl. Again, where there's smoke, there's fire, and I'm here to fan the flames.

Maddie's Minute Monologue, Freedom Awards Preview Show

-Madison Humphries

Score one for the home team, me. On July 4th, Jasmine agreed to walk the red carpet with me, even after Madison Humphries decided to base the opening of her show on some bullshit. Jasmine and I rode to my mother's house to take the limo to the Freedom Awards for Black Excellence, where I would be honored. When my mother met Jasmine in person, she hugged Jasmine so tight that I thought she might break her.

Fireworks bloomed in the night sky, to celebrate Independence Day, as I walked hand in hand with Jasmine through the throng of reporters. My mother, who didn't *'want to be bothered with all that mess'* had followed security in through a different entrance.

We met up in the lobby, and my mom pulled me aside under the pretense of fixing my shirt, while Jasmine spoke to Tisa Sparks, who was producing the show.

"Don't you mess this up for us," My mother warned, straightening my already perfect tie.

"For us?" I chuckled. "I swore it was just Jasmine and me dating."

"Call it what you want, but the way you two are out here in color-coordinated outfits, and you can't keep your eyes or hands to yourself, has me on baby watch."

"Ma," I protested. "Chill, everyone's coordinated in red, white, and blue to celebrate Independence Day. It's the Freedom Awards."

"Did you go with her to find your suit and help her find a dress or not?"

When I had no rebuttal, she went on.

"You're my handsome son," she pinched my cheek. "And Jasmine is surely beautiful. I like her. I like her with you, and I want some pretty grandbabies. Take care of her."

"You always told me to count my blessings, and I'm adding up every day that I have her in my life. I got this."

We sat on the front row of the theater's plush seats, my mother to my left, Jasmine to my right, and Kingston to Jasmine's right.

The Freedom Awards started on time, thanks to Tisa and her team, and proceeded without any glitches. The further into the show we got, the more subdued Jasmine became. I was concerned by her clapping less, no chair dancing during performances, and fewer smiles.

"Are you alright?" I inquired her during a break.

"Yes," she leaned over to kiss my cheek. "How are you? Are you excited?"

She was deflecting. She'd been quiet all night. I knew she was frustrated about Madison, even though she claimed not to be. I hoped that she didn't regret us. It had taken me so long to get her by my side finally, and I wouldn't lose her. I didn't want the outside world to break her.

"I'll be better when I'm sure you're good," I admitted, lacing our fingers together and bringing her hand close to kiss it.

"Tonight is your night. I'm only here to support you." She placed a hand around mine. "It's weird being in the front row. I'm nervous, that's all. I'm not usually this close to the important people."

I sighed, separating our hands. If nothing else, I wanted Jasmine to be at ease. My career was important to me. I'd never stop wanting to make music, but being with Jasmine only enhanced my ability to do so. I loved that I was free to be myself with her. Jasmine didn't bat an eye when I left the bed in the middle of the night to scribble down lyrics to a song. She didn't mind that I tapped out rhythms from my mind at the table or hummed melodies that no one else could hear when I drove. I didn't mind the quiet moments when she needed to focus on a script or running lines with her. I loved being with her. I loved the version of myself that I could be with Jasmine. I loved Jasmine.

Excitement and anticipation buzzed around the auditorium as the ceremony entered a brief commercial break. I sat there, soaking in the event, my hand resting lightly on Jasmine's knee. I was lucky.

As the audience began to stir, taking advantage of the break to stretch their legs or whisper excitedly among themselves, Jasmine turned to me with a gentle smile.

"I'll be right back," she said. "I need to freshen up my makeup."

I wasn't fluent in her different faces yet. I couldn't tell if she was sad or worried, but I knew something was off.

I nodded. "Okay, but don't take too long. You're the most beautiful thing in this room, and I don't want to be without you for too long."

"Ok, cheesy corn chip. I'll be quick, promise." Jasmine leaned in and pressed a soft kiss to my cheek, her lips lingering for a moment longer than necessary. As she stood up, I couldn't help but give her ass a quick smack. She looked back, and I got a glimmer of a smile.

"I got you later," she winked, disappearing into the crowd and moving towards the exits.

It was my mom's voice that brought me back to reality.

"MmHmm," she hummed. "Baby watch."

"Mom." I sighed. "Pump your breaks. I got to get her to marry me first."

I surprised myself with that but turned my head away from my mother's gleeful expression.

I watched Jasmine go, my eyes tracing the elegant sway of her hips until she was lost in the crowd. I saw Tisa Sparks, one of the producers, urgently ushering people out of the auditorium. Her movements were swift and purposeful as she guided everyone towards the exits.

"What's going on?" I asked, more to myself than anyone else.

Kingston hopped into Jasmine's vacated chair, his face breaking into a wide grin. "Man, everyone's talking about you and Jasmine."

I raised an eyebrow, curiosity piqued. "Why?"

Kingston chuckled, clapping a hand on my shoulder. "Except for Madison, they're all good things. She's finally with someone better, and you're finally settled."

I smiled, my thoughts drifting to Jasmine. "My girl is incredible, isn't she?"

"Damn, you just twinkled." He laughed.

"What?"

"Your eyes fucking twinkled, bro. That's crazy."

"Cut that shit out," I swiped at Kingston playfully, but he had already scooted away.

He continued laughing, and I felt like he was a big brother instead of my manager. "I'm proud of you. Putting yourself out there and sharing how much you care about someone with everyone is not easy, especially in the spotlight like this. But you're handling it like a pro."

"Thank you. That means a lot coming from you."

Soon, people were retaking their seats. The announcer was back with a warning.

"Tisa's closing the doors," Kingston noted, nodding towards the producer. "Looks like they're getting ready for your award next."

I glanced towards the exits. "Where is Jasmine? I hope she gets back before they shut us in."

Kingston laughed, shaking his head. "Don't worry. She's probably just fixing her makeup."

I tried to relax, but my eyes kept darting towards the doors, searching for any sign of her. I wondered if something had gone wrong. What if Dylan had shown up? What if she was more messed up over what Madison said than she acted?

I wanted her back by my side, where she belonged. I wanted her near me. I wanted her to hear my accomplishments. I wanted her to be proud of me because I was damn sure proud of her.

Just then, Tisa's voice cut through the murmur of the crowd. "Alright, folks, let's get those seats filled. We're about to go live again."

The room seemed to tighten, the energy shifting as everyone hurried to find seats.

The announcer began the countdown, and I stood.

"Where are you going?" Kingston asked.

"Gotta find Jasmine," I said quickly.

When I faced forward, Tisa was standing there with her electronic device.

"Doors are shut for this segment," Tisa said without room for argument.

She didn't know me, though, and if something was wrong with my girl, then there wasn't enough security in this place to hold me back.

"She's fine. She's backstage doing me a favor." Tisa explained. "We need you right here, honoree."

"Don't play with me, Tisa. I'll knock all this shit over." I was about to push past her when she spoke again.

"I promise you." Tisa pointed to the stage. "Take a deep breath. Your lady is just fine."

I looked up to see her moving around on the side of the stage. Just seeing her put me at ease, and it was magic.

"Thanks," I told Tisa.

"Exclusive rights to the wedding," Tisa winked before displaying a grin.

I was left confused but managed to find my seat while curiously watching as Jasmine moved around the shadowed stage.

"Did you know about this?" I asked my mom and Kingston. They had given me the names of possible presenters, but none stood out. Jasmine's name hadn't been on there.

She was impressive. Her presence alone was capable of stealing the show. The house lights dimmed, the stage lights warmed to a glow, and the room fell into an expectant hush. The spotlight illuminated the stage, and there she was—Jasmine, body making me feel like a firecracker - ready to explode. Her dress shimmered and sat just right on those breasts. For a moment, I was utterly entranced. She looked like my wet dream, and I barely registered the words she was saying.

The crowd's applause brought me back to reality, and I realized I had missed the entire skit she'd done with her *Brazen Renegade* co-star.

"Speaking about Renegades, trailblazers, it's my honor to present this next award to an incredibly talented artist," Jasmine began the introduction.

I knew what the words on the teleprompter said because they had sent them to me in advance. They were flattering but superficial. They focused on my dance moves, body, and stage presence. All great, of course, but they didn't capture the real me.

Jasmine started off reading those scripted words.

"At age thirteen, he already had two certified gold records," she paused and cleared her throat. She took a deep breath, and that's when her words differed from what I remembered reading. "But there's so much more to Graham than just his impressive dance moves and good looks."

"G-Style is a true artist in every sense of the word," she continued, warming her voice with genuine admiration. "He's written songs for countless people in this industry, collaborating on over 200 projects. His music touches lives because it's written from the heart. Beyond his music, G-Style is dedicated to giving back. He's involved in numerous charities, using his platform to make a difference. He's made a difference in how I see the world and how I feel while living in it."

A murmur of approval rippled through the audience.

I could see the tension ease from her shoulders as she spoke from her heart.

"G-Style is not just an entertainer; he's a creator and philanthropist who sponsors organizations that provide youth sports camps, college scholarships, small business loans, and housing assistance. He is a genuinely kind soul and a sexy body."

There was laughter, but I was in awe. Jasmine shared everything that I wanted her and others to see in me.

"G-Style's art isn't just about what you see on stage," she continued. "His music is the soundtrack to summers, late-night car rides, porch parties, and lovemaking. His music is about *belonging*. It's about the passion he pours into every note, every word. It's about *love*."

She paused, and I let the weight of her words sink in. She was making her speech and making a statement.

"G-Style is more than his body. He's a man who listens, who cares deeply, and who's committed to making a positive impact."

The crowd erupted in applause, and I stood up with a humble smile spread across my face. My eyes glistened with gratitude, and now I knew and understood how much Jasmine cared for me.

"Ladies and gentlemen," she revved, her voice strong and proud.

"Please join me in welcoming the one and only Graham G-Style Ward to the stage."

"That's my baby!" my mother shouted before hugging me.

The applause grew louder and swelled as I stood. Feeling a flush of heat rush to my face, I made my way to the stage, my heart pounding with excitement and nerves.

As soon as I reached her, I took the award and pulled her in for a hug.

"Thank you," I whispered.

Without thinking, I kissed her, a soft, lingering kiss meant to say everything my heart felt at that moment.

I could hear the gasps, but I held onto her. Fuck hiding. Forget worrying about anyone that wasn't us. She was mine, and we were free to love how we wanted to. A few cheers erupted from the back, but I didn't care. Kissing Jasmine and loving her out loud felt like the most natural thing in the world.

I pulled back, looking into her eyes, and then turned to the microphone. "I apologize for that," I expressed, my voice a bit unsteady. "Actually, no, I'm not sorry at all."

The crowd laughed.

"Can you all see her?" I asked, gesturing to Jasmine, who looked slightly embarrassed but was smiling, nonetheless. "Isn't she just... everything?" I took a deep breath, the words I had planned to say slipping away, replaced by something deeper, something more profound.

I looked at the award and then at Jasmine, nodding at her before I spoke.

"To paraphrase the illustrious Tupac: They like to beat us down a lot," I moved closer to the microphone to emphasize my next words. "The media and Madison like to clown a lot - but I think it's time to heal our women and be real to our women."

There was applause, but I put up a hand to quiet them.

"I know that this moment is supposed to be about me, but when you see her - see me, or you're gonna really see me, ya' feel me - and that's on Will Smith."

Laughter hopped around the space, although I was dead serious.

"Thank you to my management team and Kingston, who heads it. Thank you to Spinner Records for honoring my release. I've completed my last record for them." I had to pause about that. "I'm thankful to the woman that brought me here, my mama, and the woman that has given me a new purpose here, Jonquil Jasmine Myers."

I lifted my arm, and Jasmine moved to fall in place next to me.

"It was said that creativity is the wind that carries the soul to freedom, and love is the sky for it to soar." My voice echoed through the auditorium, and there was a perfect silence for a moment, a collective breath held in awe. "Thank you for the love that has allowed me to soar. Thank you for loving my expression of freedom."

I turned to Jasmine. "And thank you, Jasmine, for being my sky. For allowing me to soar higher than I ever thought possible." I took her hand, the warmth of her touch grounding me, giving me the courage to face whatever came next.

The crowd erupted into applause, a standing ovation that felt like a wave of love washing over our union. I smiled, pulling Jasmine closer, and together, we made our way off the stage, the sound of the applause echoing in our ears like a promise of a bright, beautiful future.

22

GRAHAM

It was the fourth of July, and I was trying to find my freedom deep in the bottom of her pussy. We were supposed to be in our seats at the Twenty-Eighth Annual Freedom Awards, celebrating Black Excellence, but I enjoyed everything about Jasmine. Her soft moans, the sensitivity to my touch, the way she was so pliable in our connection, letting me bend and move her in the most pleasurable ways.

After Jasmine and I left the stage, we bypassed the congratulators and media to slip into a private restroom. I slid a few bands to the stagehands and hall crew to keep a lookout and walked her into the very clean and modern space.

Instinctively, I went for her mouth, finishing the kiss that we shared on stage. It was passion, need, and lust, it was us. We were in constant motion, tongues, hands, pelvises, and feet finding ways for our bodies to meet.

"Let's do this shit for real, Gem," I panted against her lips. "I want us."

"You're just high off the adrenaline of tonight." She answered between licking at my lips and removing clothes.

"Possibly, but that doesn't change that I want you."

"Take this pussy," she whispered into my neck as if that was the only part of her that she had to offer.

I lifted her onto my dick, hungry for that part of her and more.

"I knew that's what you wanted." She smiled.

"I want it all." I groaned as I pushed through her slick warmth. With her legs spread and feet locked at my back, I loaded into her.

"It's. To. Soon," she whined as I stroked into her.

With every thrust, I tried to erase more remnants of her past and increase thoughts of the joy we could experience together in the future.

"Stop holding back," She demanded in a sing-song voice.

She wanted me to finish. She wanted me to prove that we were all about lust, but it was more. I wasn't giving up. If I had to do her until daylight to prove that I was down for her, that I would hold her up, I would.

"Give me my nut," She pleaded.

"Say you're mine," I answered.

I lifted her, turned my face away from me, and then drove into her from the back.

She moaned but didn't answer as I picked up the pace and pressed her ass cheeks further apart. I drove in harder.

"Shit. Um…" She stuttered. Her face was pressed tightly against the wall, which didn't help.

She flexed her pelvic muscles, clamping my dick so tight that it almost took me out. Jasmine knew what she was doing. That vice grip of hers would have me seizing.

"J… Got damn. Quit playing," I growled.

I was going to win. I was going to make her give in.

"Act like you fucking know," I punctuated each word with a thrust. "This my shit."

That did it. The last pump and a half sent her over the edge, with her singing out my name. I never wanted her song to end. Best voice ever.

Fireworks. I exploded into her, my sky, where I was free, now and forever. Rivulets of stars danced across my eyes as I hooked my arms underneath hers to grab those breasts and grind harder.

I released a guttural growl before collapsing against her back, trying to remember language.

"What if it doesn't work?" She asked between gulps of air against the wall. My legs were holding us up, but I didn't know for how long, so I released her.

"We'll always work if we both try," I explained, disconnecting from her to clean up at the sink and reapply clothing.

"What about the media? What about our careers?" she asked while reaching for her dress on the counter. She made her way over to the sink to clean up as well.

"Wait, don't answer that," She paused mid-wipe to catch my gaze. "My answer was all fear, based on the residue from hurt."

"Understandable," I started, but she interrupted.

"You have to know some things." She took my hand in hers and placed the towel down. "I'm a mess, and I'm doing the work to heal, but I'm still anxious about us. Second, I big love you. It's not some little blossoming, let-me-think-about-it kind of love; it's full love."

"I value you too much to ever jeopardize that," I emphasized, pulling her in closer as she nuzzled into my neck.

"I love you," I continued. "No matter where I am in the world, I'll represent that love with integrity. I'll honor you. We got this."

She locked her fingers in mine before repeating, "We got this."

THE END

ABOUT THE AUTHOR

SUBIRA MILES

The literal meaning of Subira is patience, and her life journey reflects the many trials she has faced and the triumphs that have rewarded her persistence, a reoccurring them throughout her work. Subira writes the stories that she wants to read and then shares them with anyone willing to listen or read them. Her stories open the door to her mind for others to experience characters that they will root for and grow to love. Her goal is to share hope through stories that make people feel good.

Subira enjoys simplicity in her spare time: Read. Write. Vibe to music. Eat good food. Repeat.

Join her on this adventure, exploring the worlds she's created and finding a piece of your own story in her penned experiences.

Instagram: SubiraMiles

TikTok: SiennaOchreBooks

Also, please be sure to check out the remaining six books of the collaborative:

Sparks in the Moment by *Juri Hines*
Freedom is Mine by *M.K. Seven*

Ignited on the Fourth by The Author Cadence James
Spar-Spangled Swagger by Kamyra Harding
Smoldering Embers Still Burn by Elle Robs
Fire & Ice by Robbi Renee ~ coming soon

ACKNOWLEDGMENTS

Thank you to my family. Writing takes time away from my moments with you and I appreciate you allowing me the space to do what I love and loving me while I worked through it.

I appreciate the ladies of the Seduction in Red, White, and Blue Collaborative, because these are some fierce women who are committed to their craft, are willing to learn, and are willing to share. The way we huddled together to support each other, not just in word, but in action, will forever stay with me. We did not always have the same view, but the common goal got us to publication. Thank you to Robbi Renee for having the vision to put this cohort together.

My sister, Ashley, is so freaking amazing. Every time I said I said "Read this", she was like "Bet". When I say, she had my back, I'm talking pep talks, plot thoughts, and character analysis. She has been a true blessing in this experience.

R.I.H to my father, who always believed in me. I am forever grateful.